"I'll take the baby."

Eric beamed, extending his hands.

Isabel hesitated, sending him a dubious, sidelong glance.

Eric reached into his coat pocket and whipped out a copy of a book on baby care. "I'm well prepared."

Isabel stared at the book, then into his face, and burst out laughing. But when she handed Kristal to him and their eyes met, her laughter ended abruptly with a peculiar little catch in the back of her throat. To think he would go to so much trouble...

She stood a moment longer, watching his large hand cup the back of the baby's head just so as he positioned her body along his arm and into a football carry.

"She won't break," Isabel pointed out, then harrumphed to chase an annoying frog from her throat.

"Of course, she won't." Eric took the canvas tote in his free hand and looked at Isabel proudly. "We'll be fine, Mom."

Dear Reader,

October is a very special month at Silhouette
Romance. We're celebrating the most precious love
of all . . . a child's love. Our editors have selected five
heartwarming stories that feature happy-ever-afters
with a family touch—*Home for Thanksgiving* by
Suzanne Carey, *And Daddy Makes Three* by Anne
Peters, *Casey's Flyboy* by Vivian Leiber, *Paper
Marriage* by Judith Bowen and *Beloved Stranger* by
Peggy Webb.

But that's not all! We're also continuing our
WRITTEN IN THE STARS series. This month
we're proud to present one of the most romantic
heroes in the zodiac—the Libra man—in Patricia
Ellis's *Pillow Talk*.

I hope you enjoy this month's stories, and in the
months to come, watch for Silhouette Romance
novels by your all-time favorites, including Diana
Palmer, Brittany Young, Annette Broadrick and
many others.

The authors and editors of Silhouette Romance
books strive to bring you the best of romance
fiction, stories that capture the laughter, the tears—
the sheer joy—of falling in love. Let us know if
we've succeeded. We'd love to hear from you!

Happy Reading,

Valerie Susan Hayward
Senior Editor

ANNE PETERS

And Daddy Makes Three

Silhouette Romance

Published by Silhouette Books New York

America's Publisher of Contemporary Romance

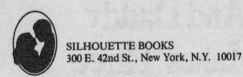

SILHOUETTE BOOKS
300 E. 42nd St., New York, N.Y. 10017

AND DADDY MAKES THREE

ISBN: 0-373-08821-3

First Silhouette Books printing October 1991

Printed in the U.S.A.

Books by Anne Peters

Silhouette Romance

Through Thick and Thin #739
Next Stop: Marriage #803
And Daddy Makes Three #821

Silhouette Desire

Like Wildfire #497

ANNE PETERS

has either lived or traveled in virtually every part of the world, but her roots are firmly planted in Pacific Northwest soil now. A mother—and grandmother—of two, she lives with her sales-manager husband in Renton, Washington. When not writing, she reads, gardens, baby-sits her grandchildren or travels—and has even been known to do housework at times.

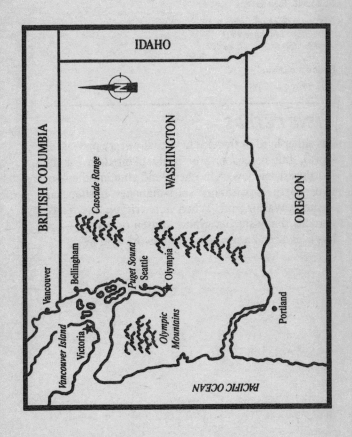

Chapter One

Eric Schwenker was no prude, but the sight of a pair of naked, not quite gleaming little buttocks less than ten feet away did, for a moment, give him pause. He stood and watched as, above the bared nether cheeks, sturdy legs kicked the air with uncoordinated vigor. They were deftly caught in one hand by the young woman who had been rummaging in a large canvas bag at her feet.

"Gotcha," she exclaimed in a mellow soprano vibrating with suppressed laughter. She raised the tiny posterior higher and swabbed it with several white squares, saying, "Hold still, you little squirmy-worm and let Mummy get you clean. There. There we are. That's better...."

The young woman crooned on while restoring the kicking and cooing infant's modesty with competent dispatch. Eric Schwenker shook his head, a kind of half-amused incredulity puckering his brow as he thought that here was a woman who took motherhood in stride and then some. The child was so small; it couldn't be very old—whatever had happened to maternity leave? Or maybe the mother was the sort of modern woman who constantly has to prove to herself, and to the world, that she is as good as or better than any man.

Eric gave a mental shudder and pitied the poor sap who had married her. Releasing the door, he stepped out into the parking lot and over to the snack truck. The men from his shop were already there, buying coffee, tea, doughnuts or muffins.

It was the morning coffee break at R. E. Schwenker Engineering, Ltd., and the young woman had ministered to her child on the front seat of the vehicle with the name Buns 'n' Java stenciled on its side. The door she'd been standing in was closed now; mother and baby were ensconced inside the cab.

Passing, Eric's quick glance took in the fact that the child was nursing. His frown reappeared. Surely there was a time and a place for everything, and just as surely, a parking lot during his shop's coffee break was neither the one nor the other.

"Can I get you anything, Mr. Schwenker?" the tobacco-roughened voice of his shop foreman, Frank Le-Fleur, called out.

Eric's frowning gaze snapped from the inappropriate but tranquil plateau in the front of the truck to the bustle of activity at its back. His foreman appeared to be playing host.

"Did you change jobs without telling me, Frank?"

Frank chuckled, a bit red-faced. "No, boss, nothing like that. I'm just helping Isabel out, this being the baby's feeding time and all...." His voice trailed off on a note of uncertainty, then firmed as he added, "I'm on my own time."

"It's all right, Frank. Never mind." Eric waved aside anything else his foreman might have felt obliged to say in his defense. "I came out here for some coffee, not to check up on you. My percolator just gave up the ghost, so how about pouring me a large cup? Two sugars and cream, please."

"That'll be ninety cents, boss." Frank handed Eric a large disposable paper cup of the black brew along with some wrapped sugar cubes and coffee creamer, then accepted the proffered dollar bill.

"Ninety cents, is *that* what it costs these days?" Eric pocketed his ten cents of change, his tone incredulous as he added, "If I recall correctly, a cup of coffee was less than half that when I first came to British Columbia."

"And when I was a boy, it was a nickel," his middle-aged and balding shop foreman replied. "Times change," he added philosophically, then squinted up at the younger man. "Guess you don't do much grocery shopping, eh?"

"Grocery shopping?" Eric couldn't remember the last time he'd set foot in a supermarket. "Why, no," he said, feeling somehow at a disadvantage. "My housekeeper—"

"Oh, yeah. Her." Frank grimaced. "The dragon lady who came charging down here with your lunch that time."

Eric laughed as he stirred the cream and sugar into his coffee. "When it comes to my well-being she can be a terror all right. Still, I'm lucky to have her looking after me, helpless bachelor that I am."

For a moment Frank looked as if he'd like to comment on that, but apparently thought better of it. "It's that damn inflation," he said, getting back to their original topic. "Drives up prices everywhere."

"Tell me about it." Eric carefully sipped. "Don't I see it here with almost every job we bid on? It's getting harder all the time to make a profit without pricing yourself out of the market. And there's always some Third World country ready to manufacture and sell almost anything for less than we can.''

Frank grunted something by way of agreement, his hands busy doling out drinks and snacks.

Eric absently watched. Ninety cents a day might not sound earthshaking in and of itself, but it would pay for a new coffeepot in less than a month. Little economies like that could make or break a small business like his. The men, too, might prefer not to squander a buck a day....

"Say, Frank."

"Yeah, boss?"

"What do you think? Would one of those large coffee urns be a good idea for the shop? If all of you chipped in to a coffee fund—"

Murmurs and exclamations of protest from the men cut short his well-intentioned suggestion. Frank's voice was the loudest. "Thanks, but no thanks, Mr. Schwenker. We like things as they are. Right, guys?"

The men chorused their agreement and, one by one, trailed back to their positions inside the shop. Only Frank remained.

"The men enjoy the truck's daily visits," he explained. "It makes a nice change for them to strut around and chat Isabel up a bit. You know."

"Sure." Eric nodded. "I can see how it would."

Actually, he saw nothing of the kind. As a rule, the men, most of them married, were huddled in groups of two and three talking hockey and knocking the government. If today was anything to go by, the woman spent the breaks tucked away inside the truck's cab with her child. Prior to her recent entry into motherhood she'd been pregnant, right? Which meant that she'd hardly qualified as flirtation material then any more than she did now.

Much more likely was the thought that had just occurred to him—Frank, whose daughter had been killed, pregnant, in a car accident a year ago, had emotionally adopted this young woman as a substitute. Coddling and helping her a little probably eased the pain of his loss. Eric had no problem with that.

He clapped the older man on the shoulder. "Anyway," he said, dismissing the coffee-urn idea, "it was just a thought."

"Well." Visibly relieved, Frank stepped around him to knock on the window of the cab. "Gotta settle up with Isabel now."

The window was rolled down. "Time?" the woman asked.

"Yup." Frank handed her the cash box and gave a brief accounting. The finances settled, he cocked his head in Eric's direction. "Thought you might like to meet Mr. Schwenker."

"Oh, your boss. Sure. Here..." She handed a blanket-swaddled bundle out through the window. "Hold Kristal a moment, will you please, while I straighten my clothes."

Watching the exchange, Eric's suspicions with regard to Frank's motives were confirmed. The expression on Frank's face was that of a doting grandparent as he gazed down at the child in his arms. Amusement warred with empathy in Eric's breast. He, too, had lost loved ones, not to death, but to geographical distance and the vagaries of world politics.

"Over the shoulder, please, Frank," reminded the baby's mother, opening the door to step from the truck. "She needs to burp." She beamed a fond smile on the pair, then turned toward Eric, who was lounging near the doughnut display.

"Good morning," she said, crisp civility firming the soft tone she'd used when addressing Frank.

Eric pushed away from the truck and shifted his cup of coffee from right hand to left while rapidly taking stock of the woman in front of him. He noted that her polite little smile exposed sparkling white even teeth, that she had clear sea-green eyes, and that her hair was an interesting mixture of gold and wheaten shades of blond. It was pulled back and hung in a thick braid halfway down her back. A bulky down vest over a man's flannel shirt obscured the shape of her body, but the long legs in faded denim looked shapely in spite of the woolen socks drooping over the tops of heavy hiking boots.

The hand she put into his outstretched one was warm and slender, its clasp surprisingly strong. He had found that most of the women he met, if they shook hands at all, did so with disconcerting limpness. Back in his country of birth, a handshake was considered something of a character reference, a firm grip indicating forthrightness and integrity.

Consequently, he should have been impressed by the sterling qualities this woman's clasp revealed, but perversely, he wasn't. He decided that, combined with her level unwavering regard, the strength of her handshake was further proof that here was a woman who obviously thought herself equal to—or more likely, better than—any man.

"R. E. Schwenker," he introduced himself.

"I'm Isabel Mott."

"I assume you took over this truck from Ron Potter?"

"That's right, I did."

Their hands unclasped, but their gazes remained on each other in mutually curious assessment. She was older than she'd appeared at first glance. Late twenties, he'd hazard, and yet, standing as near her as he was, he detected an air of vulnerability about her wide eyes and scrubbed-clean face that was completely at odds with her apparent age and assertive stance.

To be honest, on closer inspection he didn't know quite what to make of her. He'd gone through the motions of an introduction out of courtesy to Frank more than anything else. After all, he had nothing to do with the coffee truck as a rule. He ought to be getting back to work now, too. God knew he had no time for idle chitchat. Yet he made no move to go. Something about her drew him and kept him there, in spite of the fact that women of her ilk—feminists—generally turned him off. He'd been raised in an environment where women were women and men were men, and where the rules of conduct for each gender were clearly defined and observed. Everything about this woman seemed to defy those rules, and yet . . .

Isabel found the man's lengthy perusal mildly irritating, while the vibes of disapproval she felt emanating from him made her bristle. She'd just bet that air of old-world formality he wore like a starched suit went hand in glove with equally old-world chauvinism. She'd come across it before, though generally not in men so young. He'd be what? Thirty-five, thirty-six? Whatever, she was just the person to rattle the guy with some new-world sarcasm.

"R.E." She creased her brow in pretended puzzlement. "Is that a name? How do you spell it?"

"Pardon?" He looked at first nonplussed, then irritated. "They're initials. . . ."

"Initials! Of course. How silly of me." Isabel rolled her eyes and indicated the logo above the shop entrance. "And there they are on the sign, too."

She was teasing him, Eric realized with chagrin. She was using humor to make some kind of point. He didn't have to wait long to find out what it was.

"So do they call you R? Or E?"

"Neither." Catching the glint of laughter in the verdant depths of her eyes, he gave a rueful chuckle. "Forgive me, Mrs. Mott. The name is Rudolph Eric Schwenker, which seems like such a mouthful."

"You're right, it is." Isabel let her own laughter surface. "And that's *Ms*. Mott, Herr Schwenker. Or call me Isabel."

Eric was entranced by the change that laughter brought to her face. Without thinking, he said, "Would you be offended if I asked why an attractive young woman like you dresses like a lumberjack?"

"Yes, I would."

Eric saw shutters drop where just for a moment there'd been light. Damn, he *had* offended her. He cursed himself. He wasn't usually this clumsy and tactless.

"I'm sorry, it's just—" he began.

Isabel cut short his apology. "Forget it." She couldn't believe he'd actually managed to hurt her feelings. It's what she got for letting her guard down. Well, she wouldn't again. Turning to Frank, she held out her arms. "I'll take her now, Frank. We're making you late."

Eric noted that her fingers were bare of rings. Another feminist thumbing of the nose at convention? Without stopping to analyze why this should be of interest to him, he decided to find out.

He winked at the wide-eyed infant and gave its mother a conciliatory smile. "And who's this little treasure?"

Isabel's eyes, as green and cool as mint, met his. "My daughter."

"Really?" He insinuated a finger into one of Kristal's little fists. "She's beautiful. How old is she?"

"Ten weeks."

"So young." Eric tugged on his finger but, like its mother, the baby had a firm grip and held on. "And is there a Mr. Mott?"

"No."

The woman's tone was matter-of-fact; her reply raised more questions in Eric's mind than it satisfied. Then she mockingly echoed the question back to him. "And is there a *Frau* Schwenker?"

Eric thought of his mother, and his smile stretched into a grin. "Why, yes," he said, "there is."

"Congratulations." Isabel peeled Kristal's fingers from his. "Excuse us, won't you?"

Annoyed with herself for having asked a personal question when she had no interest whatever in the answer, Isabel fumbled with the truck's door.

Eric reached around to open it for her, then stepped back to give her room to secure the baby in its car seat. He watched the procedure with interest, studying the seat's design and safety features with an engineer's keen eye. "Quite a practical contraption," he remarked.

"Hmm." Isabel stepped back.

Before she could close the truck's door, he beat her to it. "Allow me."

His gallantry earned him a glower. She could open and close her own doors, thank you very much. "Goodbye, *Herr* Schwenker."

"See you tomorrow," Eric countered. "Broken coffee-pot, you know."

"I see." She rounded the hood and, opening the door on the driver's side, said, "I appreciate your patronage," in a tone that seemed to indicate quite the contrary. She sped away with the screech of protesting tires.

Eric stared after her, beset with a variety of emotions that ranged from amused consternation to wounded pride at her oh-so-cool dismissal of him. Yet, when he turned toward the gray concrete building in which his was but one of several businesses, he'd made up his mind to hold off on replacing his coffeepot.

It was two o'clock in the afternoon and time for another feeding when Isabel pulled the truck into the garage below her False Creek condominium. Smiling indulgently at the squalling bundle whose arms were flailing like an orchestra conductor's, Isabel unstrapped her from the car seat and cuddled her close. Immediately the crying stopped and the little mouth rooted against the slick nylon of Isabel's down vest.

"Patience, patience, little love," Isabel crooned with a chuckle as she slid from the truck and climbed the steps leading to the door of her apartment. Shifting Kristal into a one-armed hold, she unlocked the door and entered her home.

"Only moments now, sweetheart," she murmured, hurrying down a short hall and into the nursery she had created out of the spare bedroom. Here, delicate-pink walls were bordered at the top by a wide strip of paper on which white fluffy lambs and plump puppies chased pastel butterflies in fields of daisies and buttercups. The same pattern was repeated on the curtains, lamp shade and crib sheets, and, combined with the white wooden furniture, created a bright and cheery effect.

Isabel deposited her squirming little bundle on the changing table and quickly set about the business of unwrapping and re-diapering. Then she slipped off her down vest and tossed it out into the hall. With Kristal again in her arms, she settled in the rocker she had bought at a flea market and restored to its original beauty and comfort.

She unbuttoned her shirt and, with a sigh, leaned back against the cushions. Cradling the little body against her own, soothed by the gentle motion of the rocker, she drowsed and dreamed and savored the closeness with her child just as she had ever since its birth.

Her child. Isabel smiled, still marveling at how wonderful that sounded. She bent her head to press her lips against the downy forehead. ''My very own...''

It had been worth it, she reflected, gazing lovingly at her daughter. She had been right to follow the course she had, regardless of the pain. It was behind her, all that. She and Kristal were alone, and it was a blessing, not a hardship. But then, she'd worked hard to make sure of that, hadn't she? She was financially secure, emotionally stable—now that Arnie Mott was out of the picture—and at twenty-nine, at last reasonably mature. She had a little nest egg stashed away, owned this comfortable condominium in a fine neighborhood and operated her own business. She did her share of good works. In all, she was a veritable pillar of the community and what experts would term excellent parenting material.

How strange then, Isabel mused, that even in today's supposedly enlightened environment, there were those who viewed single mothers—especially young ones—with something like suspicion. Nor did they hesitate to pry into the whys and the wherefores—and they'd better like the explanation or else.

Well. Isabel smiled wryly. She, for one, did not explain herself to anyone and had lost a couple of customers because of it. That man, R. E. Schwenker, had struck her as the type who pried and made judgments. Dressed like a lumberjack, indeed! Warmth and practicality was what she dressed for, and if the resultant look was less than glamorous, so much the better.

The way he'd pierced her with those intense black eyes of his, as if she were some alien creature of whom he didn't altogether approve. His questions had been a bit too personal.... She smiled smugly to herself. She'd had him going there for a moment, though, hadn't she?

She spared a thought for his wife, wondered briefly what she was like, then dismissed the question with a yawn. Who cared? She was tired. And no wonder—since Kristal's birth, an undisturbed night's sleep had become something of the past. She let her lids drift down, drowsily thinking that nature hadn't been completely perverse in making *two* parents the normal state of affairs. There was something to be said at times for having a partner who could share in the work.

How had her own mother coped thirty years ago? There'd been Grandma Abby, of course, but still. And these days—how was Delly getting along? Isabel sighed and thought how strange it was, this persistent urge to go see her mother, to maybe reach some kind of understanding with her. Could having become a mother herself be causing this need to reestablish contact after...what? Thirteen years of going her own way?

At seven o'clock the next morning all was quiet at R. E. Schwenker Engineering, Ltd. Eric unlocked the door to the foyer fronting his office. The work day had not officially started yet, but he was usually there ahead of the men.

As always on entering, his heart swelled with proprietary pride. This was his, this modest suite of offices and the adjoining shop. This was the fulfillment of the dreams that might never have become reality behind the Iron Curtain—which had still been an impenetrable barrier when he'd made his bid for freedom and opportunity. He had risked much, lost much; the price had been high in terms of personal sacrifice and loneliness, but still, it had been worth it.

He stepped into the larger of the suite's two rooms and took up his customary seat behind a large drafting board. On it, partially completed, was tacked the drawing for a two-ton hoist, which was but the latest of a steadily increasing number of small hoists and cranes his company designed, manufactured and serviced.

Picking up his pencil, Eric resumed work on the drawing. In the two years he'd run his own business, he had perfected and standardized several very versatile designs that sold well. But he was always willing, as in this case, to adapt his designs to the customer's specifications when asked to do so.

Eric erased a smudged line, thinking that soon now he'd have to hire a qualified designer, a mechanical engineer like himself. He'd probably have to invest in a computer system, too. If R. E. Schwenker Engineering, Ltd. was to grow as he envisioned, he'd need to be free to devote more time to sales and management, and less to the engineering end.

Frank ran the shop as if it were his own. What a find he'd been, Eric reflected, grateful for the many breaks Lady Luck had given him. An outstanding technician, Frank had been of invaluable help with the hiring of the assorted machinists, electricians, welders and mechanics needed in an operation of this kind. Personnel, the hiring and firing end of things, were not Eric's forte. He was an engineer; he was at his best with numbers, the logic of math—

The phone shrilled. Sighing, Eric swiveled on his stool and stretched down to the desk adjacent to the board. Oh, for a secretary, he thought with a quick glance at his watch to confirm they were open for business.

He picked up the phone. "Good morning, Schwenker Engineering."

The caller was a supplier of electrical equipment who quickly launched his sales pitch. Listening with half an ear, Eric longed for a cup of coffee, and it seemed quite natural that from there his mind should wander to the woman who would supply it in about another hour. He had thought of her with quite perplexing regularity since their encounter the previous day. Perhaps it was seeing her with the baby, or witnessing Frank's obvious joy in cuddling the infant. Whatever it was, meeting her had left him with a disconcerting awareness of the elements that were missing in his life. Family. A wife, children...

The call completed, Eric forced his thoughts back to the work at hand, and the next time he glanced at his watch it was nine-fifty-nine. He craned his neck to look out the window. Had she come yet?

As if conjured up by his gaze, the gray pickup with the gleaming, steel-canopied back pulled into one of the parking stalls in front of his portion of the building. Three short blasts of the horn, and then Isabel Mott could be seen scrambling from the cab and flipping open one side of the canopy to display her trays of goodies. With a smile and a wave toward Frank, who was already trotting toward the truck—no doubt, Eric surmised wryly, to assume his duties as host—she rounded the cab to the other side and was gone from view.

His heart did a strange little hop-skip, and it was with a sense of anticipation that he straightened away from the window. He slid off the stool, reached for his jacket and umbrella on the way out the door. Damn, but a cup of hot coffee would hit the spot.

Just as on the day before, Kristal's little bottom was being re-diapered on the front seat. The capable *Ms*. Mott was bent over the infant, her own trim jean-clad derriere getting soaked by the drizzle that had shrouded everything since the night before. Vancouver, October, rain— Eric had long since learned that the terms were usually synonymous.

"Good morning." He stepped closer, using his umbrella to shelter not only himself but Isabel's back, as well. "Nasty day on which to have a baby out."

"Not so bad." Isabel didn't look up as she swiftly buttoned Kristal's fluffy sleeper and bundled her up in the blanket. "There, now, all snug as a bug," she murmured, then bent to nuzzle the baby's cheek before straightening to face him.

"Thanks for the roof." She patted her damp backside and grimaced. "Guess I'll have to come up with another way of changing the baby on days like this."

"Days like this, as you put it, will outnumber sunny days from now till spring, Ms. Mott. Wouldn't it be better to leave the child at home?"

"Hardly practical, *Herr* Schwenker, when I'm carrying her lunch in my breasts, now is it?"

Just as on the day before, Isabel's words and ironic tone managed to bring a flush to Eric's cheeks. Damn the woman. And damn himself. Why was he sticking his nose in where it didn't belong? Yet, even as he wondered he heard himself growling, "Perhaps, then, you should stay home with your child until she's old enough to be left."

"Like a good little hausfrau, Herr Schwenker?" Isabel drawled sweetly. Gathering Kristal into her arms and seat-ing herself inside the cab, she slanted him a pointed look. "Excuse me, but I need to unbutton this shirt now..."

"I'll get my coffee." Eric let the door of the truck fall shut. Cursing himself for giving a damn about this contrary female and her child, he stalked around to the other side.

The men were congregated in the large opening of the shop, consuming their beverages and snacks out of the weather. Frank was huddled beneath the awning formed by the flipped-up sides of the metal canopy, apparently tallying receipts. Noting Eric's approach, he reached for a large cup and filled it with coffee.

Money and coffee exchanged hands. Eric added cream and sugar, slurped a careful sip. He nodded a greeting to his men before he turned to his foreman with studied nonchalance. "So, Frank, how long have you known Ms. Isabel Mott?"

Frank nodded in acknowledgment of the question and held up a quick staying finger as he counted a handful of coins. "Sixty-five, seventy-five, ninety. There, to the penny, sixteen dollars and ninety cents. Looks like the guys were peckish today."

He dumped the coins onto the bills already resting in the cash box. "How long have I known Isabel?" He snapped down the lock and extracted the key. "Since she took over this truck, which must be, oh..." He narrowed his eyes and calculated. "About a year or so now, I'd say. Why?"

"I don't know." Eric shrugged, vexed by his apparent inability to leave well enough alone. "Lord knows it's none of my business, but, dammit, Frank, I hate to see that little one out here in this dampness. Since you seem to be the woman's good friend maybe you can talk some sense into her."

Frank lifted the grease-spotted ball cap he wore and smoothed a stained and calloused hand over the sparse hairs on his pate before firmly pulling the cap back down. He frowned at his boss.

"It's plain that Isabel loves that kid and wouldn't do anything to hurt it. This truck is her living, Mr. Schwenker, so what am I gonna tell her? Go on welfare?" He snorted, shaking his head. "I couldn't do it. And even if I could, you can bet she'd never go for it. That's one very independent lady in there."

"So I've noticed." Eric grimaced into his cup.

Frank chuckled, clapping him on the shoulder in a gesture of fatherly affection that did not offend the younger man. "I know how you feel, believe me, boss. That's why I'm out here doing this. There's something about her. My Jenny had it, too...."

"Right." Catching Frank's misty expression, Eric quickly raised his cup in a kind of salute and drained it. "Well, as I said, it's none of my business." Tossing the empty container into the trash, he turned toward the building. "Back to work, I guess."

Frank's nod was slow, his expression pensive. "Right."

The foreman went to settle with Isabel, and Eric started back toward his office, debating with himself. Near the door, he reached a decision. He turned and marched back to the truck as Frank was sprinting toward the shop.

He took Frank's place at the window and rapped on the glass. Isabel Mott looked up and gave him a cool nod. The child was still at her breast, but discreetly so. Isabel's shirt and the baby's blanket left only a very modest amount of creamy flesh exposed. Yet it was this spot that drew Eric's gaze, and for the briefest moment his mind conjured up an image of the mound that was hidden from view.

Chagrined, he blinked and hastened to shift his attention to Isabel's face. She was smiling, a knowing and slightly derisive smile that, once again, raised the temperature of his blood so that it heated his cheeks.

Isabel saw his embarrassment and felt strangely disarmed by it. She didn't like the feeling, didn't want to find him in any way endearing, so she rolled down the window and said, "If a nursing infant offends your sensibilities, Herr Schwenker, I can only assume that you aren't a father yet. Maybe you should stay away from mothers with babies until you are."

Eric supposed he ought to be grateful she thought him prudish rather than a lecher, but her words rankled. "I'm European, Ms. Mott," he felt compelled to respond, "and the youngest in a family of six. All my siblings were married and had children before I left my country, but even if I hadn't seen them nursing, there was ample opportunity everywhere to observe this most natural of acts."

Her arched brows and thin smile reflected doubt, causing Eric to mentally gnash his teeth. "Look," he said, "I came to tell you that there is an unused room in front of my office. It has only an old couch, a chair and an empty desk in it, but you're welcome to utilize it as a changing and feeding station over the winter months."

As he spoke, he could read surprise, distrust and, finally, refusal in Isabel Mott's clear emerald eyes. Surprise had lightened their hue; distrust darkened it. Refusal made her eyes glitter like shards of ice.

"No, thank you," she said curtly before abruptly shifting in the seat to present him with a rigidly set shoulder and a delicately curved vulnerable nape. It was the latter that caused Eric to bite back the angry retort at the tip of his tongue and to draw a deep breath instead.

"Ms. Mott," he said in his most patient tone. "I make the offer without ulterior motives and with no strings attached. You can take it or leave it, as you wish."

Snapping away from the window, he marched back into his office, all the while berating himself for butting in where he shouldn't have.

Chapter Two

In addition to Kristal's nocturnal feedings, persistent thoughts of her mother and of R. E. Schwenker and his startling offer had intermittently kept Isabel from restful sleep. Consequently, she was somewhat less than cheerful the next morning as she drove in pouring rain across Oak Street Bridge toward the suburb of Richmond.

It was going on eight o'clock, and she had two stops on Westminster Highway and four along River Road ahead of Schwenker Engineering. Perhaps by the time she arrived there the weather would have cleared. One look at the unrelieved grayness above nullified that particular notion.

Isabel heaved a sigh. She had made a deal with herself, and the upshot of it was that if it was raining when she got to Schwenker, she would accept the man's invitation to use his spare room. It was a nice, a generous offer, and even though she was loath to be beholden to anyone, particularly a man, it made no sense whatever for her to feel such extreme reluctance to accept.

Or maybe it made excellent sense. After all, if she were perfectly honest, wasn't she resisting because—God help her—in spite of everything she'd been through, there was something about this R. E. Schwenker that attracted her? Something that touched her in ways she hadn't wanted to be touched ever again? It frightened her, this subtle attraction, even though he wasn't, well, coming on to her in any way. Even though he was married.

It was that way he had of staring at her when they talked. Penetratingly, as if he were trying to see beyond the facade she presented to the world. It was a facade of toughness and reserve she had carefully cultivated and striven to keep in place at all times. It hid her uncertainties, her fears, all the emotional wounds that had been inflicted on her. Wounds, she had vowed, no one would get the chance to inflict ever again.

Isabel pressed the gas pedal nearly to the floor, squeaked by an elderly woman in a vintage sedan and whipped her truck into the lane exiting onto Number Four Road. Right now her first stop was just ahead, so she'd better keep her mind on business.

After pulling to a halt behind Johnsons's Auto Rebuilt, she checked on the sleeping Kristal. Then she gave the customary three short blasts of her horn and got out to set up shop.

"Morning, Kathy, Ed, Ray," she greeted the first arrivals, forcing cheer into her voice. "The usual? I've got blueberry muffins today, and hey, check out these oatmeal cookies. Home-baked by yours truly, and a steal at fifty cents apiece."

Business was transacted swiftly. These were union shops, so coffee breaks were of fifteen minutes' duration, and there was no time to be wasted standing in line. On rainy days like this nobody even hung around to chat, and so it was in record time that Isabel was done with the Westminster Highway stops and headed toward River Road.

Her thoughts returned to R. E. Schwenker—again. She could picture him clearly because, to be honest, she'd stared at him just as hard as he'd stared at her. He'd been easy to look at. Tall—six feet, at least. And handsome, she supposed, in a rumpled sort of way. His hair was dark, almost black and on the long side. Thick and tousled. His eyebrows matched his hair and arched just a little. His eyes were dark, and, well, penetrating was probably as apt a description as any. As if they didn't miss much. Lots and lots of lashes and a brooding sort of melancholy made them memorable.

He had the kind of looks most women probably found attractive, Isabel told herself. So what was wrong if she did, too? Just because she had no interest in men didn't mean she was dead, did it? She could still look, and even appreciate, as long as that's where it stayed. Which in Schwenker's case should be easy since the man was safely married.

So, should she accept his offer?

Isabel squinted through the streaks of grime blurring her windshield. It was still coming down in buckets out there! Nor had the deluge lessened by the time she pulled into her customary slot in front of Schwenker Engineering. What was more, the squall inside the cab of her truck was beginning to equal the one outside.

Kristal had awakened and was screaming for her second meal of the day. There were times when Isabel could swear the child had a built-in alarm clock—every four hours almost to the minute she was ready to eat. A cursory, one-handed examination found her to be soaked through to the blanket, as well.

Faced with her daughter's frantic cries, Isabel didn't spare the matter of accepting or rejecting Schwenker's offer any more thought. She unstrapped her child, grabbed up the canvas tote containing the baby's supplies and made a dash for the office. In her headlong rush she forgot to unlatch and fold up the canopy of her truck, a thought that occurred to her just as the door in front of her swung open.

R. E. Schwenker himself stood in the opening. He didn't get the chance to as much as say good-morning before Isabel thrust her bundle and her baby at him, spun around and sprinted back to the vehicle.

Frank was already there and more than willing to help set up for business.

"You know I'd never be able to manage without you, don't you, Frank?" Isabel said, securing a latch.

"Glad to do it." Frank awkwardly patted her shoulder. "I get such a kick out of you and that kid of yours."

"I know." Isabel had heard all about his daughter, and she hurt for him. "You're a good friend."

"You say that now." Frank chuckled, giving her a hand with uncovering the trays of snacks as the men began to crowd around behind him. "Used to be you'd bite my head off every time I tried to say a civil word."

"I remember." Isabel filled a large cup with coffee and added two sugars and a generous dollop of cream. "But it wasn't anything personal, you know that."

"Yeah." Frank sighed. "I'd see the bruises on your arms, and—"

"Don't," Isabel interrupted. "Please. That chapter of my life is closed. For good."

"Yeah." Frank nodded grimly. "Yeah."

Isabel motioned with the container of coffee in her hand. "I'm taking this to your boss, okay? He's inside with Kristal."

"Oh?" Frank's brows shot upward. "How'd that come about?"

But Isabel was already hurrying toward the office and didn't hear him. It had just occurred to her that she'd practically thrown her daughter at poor old R.E. Recalling his rather nonplussed expression, she couldn't help but giggle.

As she stepped through the only open door leading off the foyer, the sight that greeted her turned her lingering amusement into a loud guffaw. R. E. Schwenker was standing in the middle of the room, the bag containing Kristal's paraphernalia at his feet. Both of his arms were stiffly in front of him at a ninety-degree angle from his body. His hands were clamped beneath Kristal's armpits, and he was holding the baby just as far from himself as possible.

The expression on his face was one of bewildered dismay. "This is no laughing matter, Ms. Mott. This child has—" his nose wrinkled "—defecated."

At that, Isabel lost it completely. She plunked his coffee down on the empty desk next to the door and pressed a hand to her lips as laughter gushed up.

"I'm glad you find the situation so entertaining," Schwenker said in an aggrieved tone. "Personally, I'm a little taken aback."

"Taken aback?" Isabel gasped, straightening. "By what, the baby's bad manners?" The idea broke her up again. "Really, Herr Schwenker..." She stepped up to him, took her happily kicking and cooing daughter, and pressed a kiss on the baby's chubby cheek. "I thought you said you had nieces and such."

"I do, but..." Looking extremely discomfited, he gave a helpless shrug.

"Didn't poop in your presence, huh?" Isabel shot him a good-natured grin. "Don't feel bad—it was nothing personal. Was it, punkin?" she said to the baby, carrying her over to the desk. "Better move your coffee, Herr Schwenker. I'm about to unwrap this smelly little package."

Eric hastened to remove the paper cup, and himself, from the room.

Isabel's soft laughter followed him out the door, and he could feel the heat of a flush cover his face. Damn. He supposed she thought him a complete fuddy-duddy for the way he had acted in there. Not that he was any too proud of himself, either, but the truth was he had panicked. He'd been quite pleased to be holding the baby, and he'd been having a nice conversation with her when, suddenly, her little face had begun to turn red, then purple....

Good God, even now the remembered jolt of fear made his heart skip a beat. She's suffocating, he'd thought, frozen with horror and trying to dredge up long-forgotten first-aid procedures. But his mind had been a blank. And then, when with a rumbling sort of explosion from below, the baby's face had regained its normal hue and a telltale odor had made the situation clear, relief had nearly unmanned him. That, and the daunting realization that he was alone with the child and hadn't a clue what, if anything, he should be doing. Thank God, the mother had come....

Phew! Shaking his head, Eric expelled a puff of air. He wiped a sweaty palm on the side of his pants and pried the lid off the container of coffee. Boy, but he needed this! He sipped and made a face. The stuff was cold.

Glad to finally have a purpose, he grabbed his umbrella.

"Excuse me," he mumbled on his way past mother and child. Head bent against the wind, he trotted outside for a refill of brew and a dose of reassuring male companionship.

"Good of you to let Isabel go indoors, boss," Frank said, tossing out the contents of Eric's cup and refilling the container with fresh hot coffee. "Kid's had it rough. She can use a bit of kindness."

"Yes, well." Eric shrugged off the foreman's praise. He didn't want accolades for something that cost him nothing in terms of personal effort or money. The room had just been sitting there; it might as well be put to some use. Nor did he care to hear of the woman's troubles secondhand. Or firsthand, for that matter. Her cool and abrupt manner made it clear that any kind of sympathy would be rejected, and anyway, if she'd had it rough, well, who hadn't?

"No sense the child's catching pneumonia just because the mother prefers a man's job to a more suitable form of employment," he muttered, then reminded himself it was none of his business, he quickly changed the subject. "How's the Weston job coming along? Are we on schedule?"

"Right on time," Frank said after a short hesitation during which Eric could all but see him shifting mental gears. It was clear LeFleur was most taken by, and protective of, the redoubtable Ms. Mott. It made Eric wonder what qualities the older man could see in her that he couldn't. On the other hand, what difference did it make?

Impatient with himself, he straightened away from the corner he'd been leaning against and tossed his drained cup into the trash. "I'll see you later," he said brusquely, and marched off.

Inside the foyer, his purposeful step slowed, then stopped, as it occurred to him that in order to get to his office he'd once again have to go through the room in which she was tending the child. Damn. He frowned at the closed door in front of him. Would she mind if he came in? She would if she weren't decent. So should he knock? Wait? What?

Hell, why had he gotten himself into this? There was a pile of work on his desk and he didn't need any additional aggravation or holdup.

He gave the door a sharp rap with his knuckles. "Ms. Mott?"

"Yes?"

Just hearing and not seeing her, he was struck again by the melodic timbre of her voice.

"It's me, Schwenker," he said, mentally gnashing his teeth at his own stiffness in particular and the situation in general. This was ludicrous. He owned this place, for heaven's sake. Or, at least, he was the guy paying the rent. "Uh, I'd like to come through to my office, if I may."

"Oh." Her tone became crisp. "By all means."

Isabel opened the door before Eric could do it himself. Instinctively backing up a step, his eyes flicked to her chest. Perceiving its flannel-shirt-covered state, his gaze surged back up to hers.

She was regarding him from beneath a quirked brow with an expression that clearly indicated that his quick wayward glance had been noted. "Come in," she invited.

Eric cleared his throat. "I'm sorry if I'm interrupting. I suppose we should discuss a method by which I—"

"We're done," she interrupted, stepping aside and motioning him into the room before walking back to the sofa on which Kristal lay punching the air with her little fists. "We're just getting bundled up and ready to go."

"Well, good. Excellent." Relieved, Eric edged up next to her and peered down at the child. She was contorting her face in a huge yawn, making him chuckle. "She looks ready for a nap."

"Yes." The loving smile Isabel bestowed on her child was reflected in her voice, and it sweetened the expression she turned toward him. "Thanks for the use of the room."

"You're quite welcome." Eric was mesmerized by the change in her. "You're very beautiful when you smile," he said with warm sincerity, and instantly wished himself to the devil when her smile vanished as if it had never been.

Isabel was appalled by the surge of pleasure she'd felt beneath his admiring regard. For the barest instant she had basked in Schwenker's approval, but then sanity had rushed back. A man's approval was a fleeting thing. She'd been slow to learn that lesson, had suffered a lot of pain in the process, but learn it she had. Now, all that mattered was that she pleased herself.

"Herr Schwenker," she said, businesslike again, "if I'm going to be using this room on a regular basis, I'd like to pay you for it. What would you consider fair?"

"Why, nothing." Eric drew away, offended by the idea of accepting payment from her. "Certainly not. It's a small-enough favor."

"I don't like accepting favors." Isabel shrugged into her down vest and picked up the child. "How about free coffee for you every day?"

"No. It's not at all necessary—"

"But I insist." She walked to the door and opened it. Looking back at him, his expression of offended bewilderment made her feel ungracious and boorish. "Please," she said softly. "I'd feel a lot better."

The hint of entreaty in her voice, as well as in her eyes, instantly squelched any further protest Eric had meant to make. He could see that for some reason this was an issue of vital importance to her, and he found himself oddly loath to say something that might end their association before it had even begun.

"Very well." He expelled a resigned sigh. "You win. Coffee it is."

Her smile rewarded him. "Two sugars and cream?"

"Please."

"See you tomorrow then."

"Tomorrow," Eric said, and found himself looking forward to it.

Driving home later that day, Isabel replayed the scene at Schwenker in her mind. She chuckled. Recalling the expression of comic horror on good old R.E.'s face as he stood there holding aloft the fragrant Kristal, she laughed aloud. Poor man, no doubt he was thinking that he'd bitten off quite a bit more than he felt comfortable chewing.

As for herself, now that the matter of compensation had been resolved, she felt much better about the arrangement. The warmth and relative comfort of Schwenker's spare room today had been a far cry from the cramped and drafty cab of the truck. And really, good old R.E. was not a bad sort of man. Quite nice, actually.

So was Arnie, in the beginning.

Isabel's jaw tightened. Much as she'd like to, she couldn't deny the truth of that little reminder. In the two months preceding their quickie wedding, Arnie Mott had been the very model of solicitude and helpfulness.

And why wouldn't he have been? she demanded with an inward snort of disgust. *He never did have a job!*

This time her chuckle had to do with gallows humor instead of mirth. Arnie had moved in with her and made like a househusband, doing her laundry and cooking her meals for only one reason: he needed a meal ticket and she'd been it. She had suspected as much, but hadn't minded. It had felt so good to be spoiled and looked after for a change. In fact, she could remember thinking that Arnie was everything she wished her father had been.

Oh, boy... Isabel shook her head at her own naïveté, and thought, talk about having to be careful about what you wished for. No sooner had the knot been tied when Arnie became *precisely* the kind of man her father had been.

Lips compressed in a straight line, Isabel jerked the steering wheel sharply to the right, swinging the truck into the steep driveway leading down to her basement garage. All of which, she grimly concluded, should make it everlastingly clear to her that people were rarely what they seemed.

"Uh, excuse me, miss."

Eric felt decidedly out of place in this colorful store. It seemed every item of inventory in Mother Hubbard's Cupboard, every bed, chair, lamp or blanket, was tiny, ruffled, or painted in primary colors, and in some cases all of the above. Self-consciously looking around, he noted that all the other patrons were women, either mothers with children or mothers-to-be. Was there a rule against males frequenting the place?

"Ma'am, if I could have your assistance, please?"

He'd raised his voice a bit that time and several heads turned to eye him with curiosity. He returned their stares with what he hoped passed for a nonchalant grin while noting with relief that the clerk was among those now looking his way. Not only looking. Her face wreathed in smiles of welcome, she was at his side in seconds. "How can I help you, sir?"

"Well, now—" Eric cleared his throat "—I need to make some purchases. But I'm not married, you see...."

The clerk's smile became positively incandescent. She fluttered her lashes. "Ye-e-s...?"

"...yet I've recently acquired an infant," Eric added, oblivious to the now dimming smile. "In a manner of speaking, that is. I'd like to buy a few practical items for a nursery of sorts."

"A crib?" the clerk prompted. "Things of that nature?"

"Well, no. Accoutrements, actually." He looked around, frowning. "Perhaps a . . . a blanket kind of thing on which the child could be, you know, tidied."

"A changing pad, you mean?" She moved away to a shelf and held one up. "Like this?"

Eric beamed. "Exactly. But a blanket, as well, I think. And this." He picked up a pink, stuffed terry-cloth lamb. "And that thing." He pointed.

"The mobile?" The clerk identified the colorful contraption of ducklings and fishes suspended on strings.

"Yes." Eric nodded. "The mobile." Little Kristal would enjoy looking up at it while she nursed, he supposed. "By any chance do you have any literature on infant care?" he went on. "Perhaps a book?"

"Of course." The clerk's smile had gradually shifted from flirtatious to accommodating after a brief stop at disappointed. "New fathers find *Dr. Spock's Baby and Child Care* very helpful. Moms, too," she added, leading the way to a shelf of books and publications. "Perhaps, though, you'd like to browse a bit while I get the rest of your stuff put together."

New fathers. The term, as applied to himself, might be erroneous, but Eric quite liked the way it sounded. He preened a little beneath the indulgent glances some of the other women in the store were sending him. He pretended to browse, riffling through this magazine, that book. But he was thinking that maybe it was time he gave some serious consideration to marriage, and a family of his own.

The glimpses he'd caught of Isabel in the various acts of caring for her child these past couple of weeks had awakened a longing in him. He'd caught himself wanting to share in that caring, which was why he was giving up part of his Saturday shopping this way. With a bit of this and that, the barren spare room would be much more *gemütlich*—cozy—for mother and child, and should the need for his assistance arise, well, a man didn't like to make a fool of himself more than once, did he?

Eric picked up the Dr. Spock book, and skimmed some of its contents. "Babies aren't frail," he read. Well, that was a relief to know. He'd wanted to ask Isabel if he might hold the child again, but after the fiasco he'd made that first time he'd been afraid to. What if he hurt the baby?

"Diapers," he read. And, according to the diagram in this book, folding them looked simple enough. He was an engineer, after all—squares and triangles were shapes he could manage in his sleep.

"I'll take this book," he told the clerk, decisively snapping it shut and handing it to her. "Also a box of cloth diapers, some cornstarch powder—" preferable to talcum, he'd just read "—and some wipes."

Pulling his billfold out of an inside pocket, he trailed her up to the cash register with a confident step. As always, he thought, congratulating himself, with a little preparation and research even the most daunting of challenges could be met.

When Isabel trotted over to the building with Kristal on Monday morning, she saw that R. E. Schwenker was once again ensconced in the front door.

"Frank didn't come in to work today," he called out when she was still several feet away. "If you like, I could take charge of the little one while you take care of things out here."

"You'll what?" Isabel's eyes widened in amazement. She stopped in front of him and made a show of banging the heel of her hand against the side of her head as if to clear an ear. "Did I hear you say you'll take the baby?"

"You did." He beamed, extending his hands.

Isabel hesitated, sending him a dubious sidelong glance. "What if she's smelly?"

"No problem." Eric whipped the by now dog-eared copy of *Dr. Spock* out of his coat pocket. "I'm well prepared."

Isabel stared at the book, then up into his face, and burst out laughing. "You slay me." But when she handed Kristal to him and their eyes met, her laughter ended abruptly with a peculiar little catch in the back of her throat. To think he would go to so much trouble...

"Thank you," she said.

"You're welcome."

And somehow they both knew that through this small five-word exchange of hackneyed pleasantries a wall between them had been scaled.

She stood a moment longer, watching his large hand cup the back of the baby's head just so as he positioned her body along his arm and into a football carry.

"She won't break," she pointed out, then harrumphed to chase an annoying frog from her throat.

"Of course she won't." Eric took the canvas tote in his free hand and looked at Isabel proudly. "We'll be fine, Mom."

"Yes." For all of a heartbeat their gazes meshed, then Isabel gave a quick nod and sprinted back to the truck. Her thoughts were all questions. What should she make of his actions? What had prompted them? And how did they make her feel? As she waited on her customers, talking and laughing with them, one more question joined the list. Why was it that around R. E. Schwenker all the defense mechanisms she'd worked so hard to erect always threatened to malfunction?

Still puzzling over that at the end of the shop's break, she walked over to the building. At the door of "her" room, she froze in the act of entering, immobilized by the incongruous sight of Schwenker diapering her daughter. He did so slowly and carefully.

Next to Kristal's head, and held open by a box of baby wipes, lay the book he'd shown her. Forehead creased in concentration, he glanced at it every now and then as if to make sure he was still on the right track, all the while murmuring unintelligible things to which Kristal responded with happy gurgles.

As Isabel watched, spellbound, he caught the baby's flailing limbs and gently stuffed each one into sleeves and leggings. He ended his ministrations by wrapping her in the blanket like a priceless gift.

Scooping her up, he exclaimed a triumphant, *"Bitte, kleines Fräulein,"* and Kristal squealed her delight as he cuddled her close. "Such a sweetheart you are," he murmured.

The previous turmoil of Isabel's emotions was nothing compared to what she was feeling now as she slowly advanced into the room. She wanted to laugh; she wanted to cry, to protest, to…praise. But, "Here's your coffee" was all she said.

Eric lifted glowing eyes to hers. "I've changed Kristal's diaper," he announced with an air of triumph.

"So I saw."

"You did?" He chuckled and looked down at the child in his arms as if he'd personally just created her. "I managed pretty well, I think, considering. The doll I borrowed from my neighbor's little girl for practice wasn't nearly so wiggly." He held Kristal out to her. "We're ready for lunch now, Mom."

Isabel set the paper cup down on the edge of the desk, which, she noticed, had been transformed into a changing table complete with pad and blanket, as well as a precisely folded and aligned stack of cloth diapers. She accepted the baby, frowning, and hugged her tightly in response to a primitive and powerful surge of possessiveness. She'd been the only one to minister to Kristal's needs until now. How dared he trespass?

"You even bought diapers," she said, a note of accusation creeping into her voice.

"Cloth, you'll notice." Eric was too pleased with himself to take notice of her tone.

"Why?"

He shrugged. "You didn't strike me as someone who'd use the disposable kind. Pollution—"

"That's not what I meant," Isabel interrupted. "Though you're right, I don't. I want to know why you're doing this."

The fact that Isabel was upset finally registered and took Eric aback. "Doing what?" he asked, frowning.

"This." Isabel made a sweeping gesture that encompassed the desk, the cushions, the toy on the couch, as well as the mobile she'd just spotted. "All of this. Everything. Why? What's in it for you? What do you want from me?"

"What's in it for *me?*" Eric stared at her, tense now and angry.

Isabel clutched Kristal more tightly. Unconsciously stepping back a pace, she braced herself for a blowup. She had pushed him too far, she thought. He'd been helpful and kind and she was shoving that kindness right back down his throat. Well, fine, she thought, dredging up some self-righteous defiance. She'd known this had been too good to be true. So let him yell. Let him show his true colors. Words couldn't hurt her, and afterward she'd be able to get back to the way things had been before he'd butted into her life making like a do-gooder.

"What do you want from me?" she repeated, cursing her voice for the tremor it held, and herself for feeling both fear and regret.

Eric stared at her a moment longer. He took in her challenging stance, as well as the puzzling flicker of alarm in her eyes. He forced himself to relax.

"What do I want from you?" he repeated slowly. He paused, smiling, then drolly said, "Free coffee?"

Chapter Three

"What?" Isabel stood motionless, eyes wide. To see a man's mood change so quickly from anger to amusement was not in the realm of her experience.

"The price we agreed upon was free coffee," Eric elaborated, puzzled by the look of relief in Isabel's eyes, but wondering even more at the expression of fear it had replaced. For just a heartbeat she'd looked as if she were ready to run but then willed herself not to. For heaven's sake, why? What had she thought he'd do, strike her?

Good God. He blinked, horrified but trying not to show it as he realized that had been exactly what she'd thought. The look had been too stark, too real, for him to have imagined it. But she wouldn't thank him for letting on he knew, and so he forced a flippant grin.

"Coffee with two sugars and cream," he quipped. "And no reneging, lady."

She only stared at him, but he could see her relaxing. He allowed himself to grow serious. "There's no ulterior motive, Ms. Mott," he said. "The room is here, unused, and as to the rest..." He shrugged. "A bit of selfishness on my part, if you will. I have no family here—"

"You have a wife," Isabel reminded him.

"What? Oh. Well, of course," Eric blustered, caught off guard, "my wife."

He cleared his throat. He'd forgotten about that. He debated coming clean, but in view of her wariness decided against it. "Yes, well. I meant no children, no extended family..."

"Your wife's not from here, either, then, I take it?"

"Uh, no." Eric frowned, more and more uncomfortable with what had seemed no more than a harmless fib at the time. "No, she isn't. Anyway," he rushed on, "it gives me great pleasure to make things a bit more comfortable for you and the baby. But if it offends you—"

"No, no. It doesn't. Really." Isabel, shamed by her suspicions in the face of his obvious sincerity and caring, hastened to reassure him. The only reason she'd jumped on the poor guy in the first place was that generosity and caring weren't something she was used to in a man. With the possible exception of Frank LeFleur, that was. So, was R. E. Schwenker like Frank then? Dared she relax around him, let down her guard?

She glanced at him. He looked troubled, and she was touched again by that hint of melancholy in his eyes. He'd been nothing but kind to her, she admitted with chagrin, not proud that for the most part she'd been barely civil. She took a deep breath. "I'm sorry for the way I acted—"

"Oh, no. Please. There's no need to apologize," Eric said quickly, his own conscience tweaking him. "Let's forget it, okay?"

"Okay." Isabel felt something warm begin to kindle inside of her, and another chink break out of her wall of defenses. "Thanks."

"You're welcome."

Gradually, the spare room was more and more transformed from its sparsely furnished austerity into something resembling a combination living room and nursery. The brightly colored mobile dangling above Isabel and Kristal's customary spot at one end of the couch had been joined by a couple of cheery pictures on the freshly painted wall across from them, and several more toys had appeared, as well. In spite of the fact that most of these additions and beautifications were clearly geared toward babies, when Isabel protested, R. E. Schwenker flushed but staunchly maintained that he was doing them because he was about to hire a secretary.

"The way this business has grown," he explained, "I'm going to have to have help before too much longer. This will be the secretary's office. But don't worry," he hastened to assure Isabel, "you two won't be evicted. We'll figure out something."

He was straddling the room's only chair, arms folded on top of its backrest, and grinning with almost boyish delight at Isabel seated on the couch.

"Prosperity at last, Ms. Mott. And does it ever feel good. Did I tell you I'm having curtains installed, both here and in my office?"

"Several times. And I'm impressed." Isabel found his enthusiasm oddly endearing. "Next, I suppose, you'll be buying a Mercedes."

"'Fraid not for a while. Mechanical engineers don't come cheap, and I desperately need to hire one of those, too. Now—" he pointed at the swatches of material he had earlier tossed into Isabel's lap "—which cloth do you think will make the most attractive curtains for these rooms?"

"But that can't be up to me!" Isabel protested. "What about your wife? I mean, shouldn't you consult with her on this?"

"My wife?" For just an instant Eric was at a loss again, then, barely stifling an oath, he remembered. Was this imaginary spouse of his destined to creep into every conversation he had with Isabel? He'd tell her the truth, right now, by God.

"Look here, Isabel," he began, but then a quick look at her reminded him that though they'd become friends of sorts over the past few weeks, she never seemed completely at ease in his presence. She always looked ready to run, and that reserve of hers determinedly kept him at arm's length.

"For the moment this is your room," he went on smoothly, as if he'd never intended to say anything else, "and I'd like you to choose the material for the curtains."

"*My* room?" Isabel exclaimed. "Really, Herr Schwenker, I can't possibly—"

"Will you stop that!"

Eric leapt to his feet so suddenly his chair toppled. Isabel's mouth froze in the shape of an unvoiced "Oh!" as she stared in shock at the red-face fury of this usually even-tempered man.

"I'm sick of hearing you call me Herr Schwenker, do you know that?" Abruptly, he turned his back and stalked to the window. Hands thrust into the pockets of his pants, shoulders rigid, he stared out into the parking lot.

Isabel stared, perplexed, at the wide expanse of back with which he presented her. "I beg your pardon," she finally said, stiffly. "I didn't realize it offended you. I just thought it sort of fit you better than *Mister* Schwenker."

He spun around and glared at her. "And what is wrong with calling me by my first name, I'd like to know?"

"Why, nothing's wrong with it!" Isabel's tone heated to match his. "As a matter of fact, I seem to recall that the first time we met I said, 'Call me Isabel.' But did you? Oh, no, not until today. Which is why I assumed you preferred being formal." She sniffed. "Europeans do, I'm told."

"Horse apples!"

"What?" Isabel stiffened and gripped Kristal more tightly.

"You heard me."

Their eyes clashed, hotly dueled. The air between them snapped and crackled with tension. His eyes were like live coals, dangerously glowing. Clenching her teeth, Isabel inwardly shrank from him, even though she didn't move a muscle. Here it comes, she thought, and steeled herself for the explosion. She held her breath—then shakily expelled it as she realized with a sort of incredulous shock that the corners of Eric's mouth had begun to quiver. The blaze in his eyes flickered and was reduced to sparks of humor. He was laughing.

Relief swamped her, and suddenly she was laughing with him.

Eric sobered first. He raked a hand through his perpetually tousled mane, letting his fingers rest on the back of his neck as he stared at the ceiling and expelled a hard breath. "I'm sorry." Dropping the hand, he shot Isabel a rueful glance. "That was uncalled for."

"Oh . . . horse apples." Isabel borrowed his words to impatiently wave his apology aside. "Frankly, I'm glad we're finally going to be on more casual terms—Rudolph."

"Uh-uh." His grin was immediate and of incredible wattage. "Not Rudolph."

"No? What then? R.E.? Rudy?"

"Neither." His grin faded into a frown. "I'd like it if you called me Eric," he told her softly, wanting to hear Isabel say the name by which his family called him. Though he couldn't have said why, and though he'd never invited any of his other friends to use the name, it would somehow mean a lot to him if she did.

"Oh." Feeling as though she were drowning in the fathomless depths of his coal-black eyes, Isabel swallowed. Her heart oddly fluttered. "Oh, all right then...Eric."

A charged silence followed, one during which Isabel found it impossible to interpret the expression in his eyes nor to tear her own away. All manner of unsettling emotions sprang to life inside her. Her heart drummed against her rib cage suddenly, as though she'd just ran a race. Kristal squirmed against her tight hold. The baby's howl of protest effectively shattered the charged silence in the room.

As if stuck by a cattle prod, Isabel leapt to her feet. "It's late," she mumbled into the baby's shoulder. "I've got to run. 'Bye."

She snatched the canvas tote off the couch and was halfway out the door when Eric's warm voice stopped her.

"Isabel."

Feeling foolish, Isabel forced down the urge to keep right on running. Doorknob in hand, she slowly turned and forced herself to look at him. "Yes?"

"Your jacket." His eyes were dancing.

"Oh." *This is too ridiculous,* she fumed. *Stop acting like an idiot.* She took a deep breath, pasted on a smile and held out her hand for the down vest. "Thanks."

Eric shook his head, grinning. She really looked adorable when she was flustered, he thought. Not at all the oh-so-cool, I-don't-need-anyone Ms. Mott she liked the world to see, but rosy-faced and—incredibly—touchingly shy. He felt a rush of tenderness.

"It's cold out there," he murmured. "Turn around—I'll help you on with it."

Isabel thought fleetingly of refusing, but how would that look? "Th-thank you."

She dropped the bag onto the floor, slid one arm through the arm hole, shifted Kristal to her other side, and got the second arm through. She picked up the bag again, prepared to continue her rapid exit, but was held in place from behind by the clasp of strong hands on her shoulders.

"Bye-bye, Kristal," Eric's deep and mellow voice crooned in the vicinity of Isabel's ear. She stood stock-still, holding her breath, but nevertheless the scent of his after-shave filled her nostrils. His hands on her shoulders, the warmth of his chest almost touching her back, made her knees go weak. She shuddered as his cheek ever so slightly grazed hers while he leaned across her shoulder and pressed a kiss onto the baby's forehead.

The second he released her and stepped away, Isabel bolted. At the truck, she all but tossed Kristal into the car seat. She fastened the straps with hands that shook, then made the mistake of looking at the office windows as she rounded the hood to the driver's side. R. E. Schwenker stared back at her, frowning, and the fact that he now looked every bit as unsettled as she felt didn't reassure Isabel a bit.

That night, in bed and sleepless, she tried to analyze her puzzling reactions to what had surely been a perfectly harmless situation. She and . . . Eric were friends by now, weren't they? It wasn't as if he ever acted in any way improper toward her. On the contrary. He was often almost too polite, treating her with that touch of old-world formality she'd noted when they'd first met.

Sure, he touched her now and then—he'd take her hand, clasped her shoulder while walking her to the door. They were casual touches that seemed as natural to him as breathing. She'd come to accept them, had learned not to feel threatened by them. Which just made her sudden and unnerving awareness of him all the more ridiculous. Why, even now, thinking back, her heart started pounding again.

Isabel popped up in bed and pressed both hands to her burning cheeks. It was, she decided dismally, the way he had sounded when he'd asked her to call him Eric. As if it really mattered to him. A lot. And the way his eyes had gotten when she'd said his name. All focused and intense, as if she'd just done something wonderful. Yet, he often looked at her like that. Hadn't she decided it was just his way and not to worry about it? Yes, but ... it'd been different somehow today.

Isabel pounded the mattress with both fists. Darn it, the whole thing was as infuriating as it was bewildering, and she wished to heck she could just leave it alone.

What had gotten into her, anyway? In all of her thirteen or whatever years of physical maturity, no male, not even Arnie Mott in the course of their brief but pleasant courtship, had ever been able to raise her temperature as this man did without even trying.

This *married* man, Isabel reminded herself with a groan. Which made him off limits even if she were crazy enough to want to get involved with a man again, which she wasn't.

She plopped down on her back again and stared at the ceiling. This had to stop, she told herself sternly. If she was to continue accepting the man's hospitality, she'd have to stop looking for deeper meanings and hidden motives in his every action. R. E. Schwenker was a married man, and she was a woman who'd been burned and who'd learned her lesson. Surely they had every reason to stick to being casual friends and no more.

Eric, too, had been giving himself severe talkings-to throughout the remainder of the day. What did he think he was doing? he kept demanding of himself. Had he lost his mind? Asking Isabel Mott to call him Eric, was he crazy? She was barely even a friend, for heaven's sake. She *tolerated* him. And that only because she had need of his spare room. She made no bones of the fact that she held the male species in contempt. Had that become some sort of challenge to him all of a sudden?

Eric snorted. Hardly.

He poked at the salad his housekeeper had left for him and finally pushed it aside. He had no stomach for food. He tried to work, but that was no good, either. He tossed down the pen in disgust, stared moodily out the fog-shrouded window for a moment, then resolutely got to his feet. There was only one thing that would alleviate some of this restlessness, and that was a good run.

He quickly changed clothes and loped out into the night. The air was saturated with moisture and heavy to breathe. Soon Eric was panting, then coughing. Hell. He slowed his pace to a jog, then slowed it still more to a walk.

In front of him a young couple strolled with their arms around each other. Their heads—hers sporting a short spiked cut, his a flowing mane—were touching, and so were their lips every time they stopped talking. Now and then they softly laughed.

Trailing behind them, Eric felt a stab of envy at their happiness. He, too, wanted to be like that young man, half of a couple. In tune with someone. Nor was tonight the first time he'd felt that way. He was thirty-six, his business was established. He was ready to settle down with the right woman.

Which, of course, was the hitch. The right woman for him might be out there somewhere, but she was proving to be damn difficult to find, his expectations being what they were.

Archaic, his friend Mike Sloan called Eric's criteria, adding that today's woman no longer needed to be content with being a stay-at-home. She had a mind, she had opinions, and she had every right to exercise both.

Which was all well and good. The last thing Eric wanted was a wife without intelligence. It was the way she put that intelligence to use where he had a problem. Spare him the single-minded career woman; not for him the upwardly mobile business type, the budding executive clawing her way up the corporate ladder. What he wanted was an old-fashioned girl, one for whom he and, eventually, their children would be the most important thing in the world. One who dressed like a woman, worked in a woman's job and acted like a woman. Demure, loving, sexy...

In other words, Eric summed up grimly, a woman not even remotely like Isabel Mott.

He kicked at a bottle cap and, with a muffled curse, sent it skittering into the gutter. So why did he have so much trouble remembering that whenever Isabel Mott was around? Because he was a fool, that was why. And because he'd been so damned buried in work lately he hadn't taken the time to go out on a date.

Spotting a phone booth on the other side of the street, he made up his mind to do something about that right then and there. He fished around in the pouch pocket of his hooded sweatshirt, came up with a quarter and jauntily tossed it up in the air. Deftly catching it, lips pursed in a silent whistle, he jogged across the street.

The clank of the coin dropping into the slot of the pay phone seemed like a bell tolling in better times. He tapped out familiar digits and counted the whirring rings. On the fourth a sultry voice spoke a brief message.

Eric's lips curved in a smile of anticipation as he said, "Marcia? It's Rudy. Listen..."

In spite of her resolutions and well-rehearsed casual air, a giant boulder seemed to drop from Isabel's shoulders when, on arrival at Schwenker next morning the man himself was out. Making sales calls, Frank told her.

With the spring in her step thus restored, Isabel all but skipped into the spare room. After changing the baby, she gave in to a sudden compulsion to see Eric's office.

Once there, she made herself comfortable in the swivel chair behind his desk and began to feed her child.

Across the desk in front of her stood the high, large drafting table with its stool pushed underneath and out of the way. In the otherwise cluttered office, this small attempt at creating order was rather endearingly amusing to Isabel.

"What a mess!" she exclaimed to herself, looking around. Everywhere, on the floor, on the desk, in and on the gray metal file cabinets, rolled-up drawings, stacks of papers, files and books reposed in frightening disarray. Good grief! However did the man find anything when he needed it?

"Hel-lo, what's this?" Isabel swung her feet off the desk and scooted the chair closer. She pushed aside some drawings and looked at the two framed photographs she'd unearthed. One was of a dark-haired older woman who looked so much like Eric it just had to be his mother. Unsmiling, she had that same look of stern brooding to which he was prone, though her eyes held none of the passion mixed with sadness that made Eric's so remarkable.

"Ugh." Isabel set the photo down with a delicate shudder. "This woman looks like she'd be some formidable mother-in-law."

The other photo depicted five couples and an assortment of children who, Isabel deduced, no doubt were Eric's brothers and sisters with their offspring. None of the sisters bore even a passing resemblance to R.E., though one of the nephews looked as he must have as a little boy. Round-cheeked and gap-toothed, and with mischief written all over his face.

The phone rang. Isabel pushed away from the desk and swivelled around in an effort to locate and answer it. Three more rings had shrilled before she traced the apparatus into one of the drawers of the desk, and just as she pulled it open, Eric's velvet-over-gravel voice spoke.

She jumped like a child caught playing where she shouldn't before she realized that the voice came from the message device on the telephone.

"Good morning," it said. "This is R. E. Schwenker Engineering and we thank you for calling. We are not able to speak with you right now but will return your call as quickly as possible. Please leave your message after you hear the beep."

Isabel rolled her eyes. She would have to speak to R.E. about this message. It was sorely lacking in originality, and his slight accent made it sound stilted.

"Rudy? It's Marcia."

Rudy? Isabel snapped upright. And who the heck was Marcia? His wife?

"I got the message you left last night and, yes, I'd love to get together this weekend. I'll be home the rest of the day, so call back anytime. Ciao."

Ciao? Using her foot, Isabel slammed the drawer shut. That message did not sound like a wifely one to her. This brought two scenarios to mind. One: Herr Schwenker was a blatantly philandering husband. Or, two: he was not married.

Her mind rejected the first out of hand. She might not be the most perceptive judge of male character, but something told her that a married R. E. Schwenker would be a faithful R. E. Schwenker.

Which left her with alternative number two. Of course. She smiled grimly, nodding to herself. Things were beginning to make sense at last. Like the little incident with the draperies. No wife would countenance having another woman, a casual acquaintance of her husband's, pick out his office decor, and she'd make sure he knew it.

Isabel could hardly bear to wait till Kristal was full to have her suspicion confirmed. She was still rubbing the baby's back in hopes of a burp as she hurried out into the parking lot. Frank was just closing everything up.

"Fifteen dollars today, my girl," he announced proudly, holding his hands out for Kristal. "Let me have her a minute. Yeah, come to Uncle Frankie, love—"

Isabel plunked the baby into his arms without ceremony. "Frank, I've got to ask you something."

Frank was pressing his unshaven cheek against Kristal's silky one, eyes half-closed, swaying gently from side to side. "She's getting bigger, Isabel. And what a little beauty."

"Frank—"

"So ask. What?"

Isabel debated briefly if a sort of veiled, back-door approach might be preferable, then blurted, "Have you ever met *Mrs.* Schwenker?" before she could stop herself.

"Heck, no—the boss's mother?" He looked bewildered. "She's over there in Europe somewhere, isn't she? How could I have met her?"

"You couldn't have, of course. How silly of me." *Cute, Schwenker.* "Why did I think he was married?"

"Beats me. Though I'll bet he could've been if he'd wanted to." Frank chuckled with an air of masculine appreciation. "That man's had some mighty fine-looking women hanging on his arm at some of the company do's we've put on. Oo-ee!" Catching Isabel's cool stare, he flushed and coughed. "Uh, why're you asking?"

"Oh—" Isabel shrugged and gave a careless wave of the hand "—a Marcia called for him...."

"Marcia, huh? 'Fraid I can't help you there, girl."

"Hey, it's not important. Here—" she reached for her daughter "—I'd better let you get back to work. Thanks, Frank."

"Any time." He loped off with a wave.

Isabel stood a moment, thoughtful, then went to fasten Kristal into her seat. She checked the canopy, got into the truck and drove away, her mind on what she'd just learned. Did it change anything? Should it? Now that he wasn't safely married, could they still be friends?

Could they be more than friends?

For a moment her heartbeat accelerated, and something hot and itchy fluttered in her stomach. But then she thought of the sultry-voiced Marcia and a new but distinctly unpleasant sensation replaced the flutter. Rather than examine its meaning, she quickly went back to the original question and answered it.

Of course they could still be friends. Because where she was concerned nothing had changed. She had no interest whatever in a romantic kind of relationship, and— Whoa!

Isabel cringed. She was getting a little ahead of things here, wasn't she? Romantic kind of relationship? What was she thinking? The fact was that R.E. had invented a wife strictly for *her* benefit. Surely that was a clear indication of what he wanted, and romancing her wasn't it. No man made up a wife if he had any kind of designs on a woman.

Grimly, Isabel floored the gas pedal and shot through the intersection on a yellow. She'd just bet R. E. Schwenker hadn't invented a wife to hold off that Marcia person.

Chapter Four

Eric was gone for several days, but Isabel stayed out of his office. She hadn't decided how to handle this "no wife" thing of his, and thought maybe she'd just ignore it. Why say something when it really didn't change anything as far as their dealings with each other were concerned?

Why? Isabel pushed Kristal's stroller rapidly down the sidewalk. Because she'd like to see R. E. Schwenker squirm a bit, that was why. And then she'd like to hear him try to explain.

She was all but gasping for breath, so energetic was her walking. She had intended to meander leisurely down international Robson Street for this mild and sunny Thursday afternoon, not engage in a footrace, for Pete's sake. Terrible, the way thinking of R. E. Schwenker could raise her blood pressure these days.

She resolutely banished him from her mind and forced her feet into a more moderate pace. She was out to win-

dow-shop, as well as to give herself and Kristal a breath of
fresh air before the next rainstorm rolled in.

So enjoy it, she told herself and stopped to admire a suit
in a boutique window. Critically eyeing its classic lines, she
decided it'd look good on her. She searched for the price
tag, reared back when she saw it, and walked on with a
shrug. Where would she wear a thing like that, anyway?

The aroma of freshly ground coffee enticed her to savor a cup, and throwing caution to the winds, she splurged
on a cream puff, as well. She fed Kristal little licks of
cream, gave her some apple juice in a bottle, and then
strolled on.

The display window of an art gallery drew her like a
magnet. It was always like that. She could never pass one
without stopping to look. Today was no different. With a
quick and practiced eye she scanned the still lifes and
landscapes, then froze. There, that little watercolor seascape on the easel . . .

Without conscious thought, Isabel pushed the stroller
into the store.

"Good afternoon," a bearded young man said in greeting.

Isabel's reply was absentminded. She went straight to
the easel, looked for the familiar signature. "K."—there
it was.

"That's a Kant," the young man drawled immediately
behind her. "A fairly recent one we were lucky to get our
hands on."

"Oh?" Isabel reluctantly turned from the painting to
face the clerk. "What makes it special?"

"Why, the fact that she rarely paints these days, of
course." He said this as if it was common knowledge, but
to Isabel it was news.

"She's retired?" she asked, some nebulous dread making it suddenly difficult to speak.

The clerk looked her up and down, then visibly dismissed her as a potential customer. "Arthritis," he said, turning away.

"I'll take it." Isabel was too stunned by what she'd just heard to be offended by the man's attitude and the openly skeptical appraisal he was once again giving her well-worn outfit of jeans and oversize windbreaker.

"The price is four hundred dollars, you know."

Isabel would have bought it at any price, though she couldn't have said why. In all the years since she and her mother had parted, she had always kept an eye out for Delly's paintings, but she'd felt neither the need nor the desire to ever own one. Today it seemed imperative she have this picture, almost as if suddenly she needed a tangible piece of her mother to hold on to before it was too late. Arthritis...

"I'll take it," she repeated, rummaging in her carryall for her checkbook. Her throat felt tight, sore. Arthritis. The word kept sounding in her head like a dirge. Delly had arthritis. Her mother, whose art had been her greatest joy—her *only* joy, Isabel had come to think. And now she might not be able to paint anymore.

Isabel's hand shook a little as she made out the check. She stood silent as the little seascape was carefully wrapped. Her heart was heavy with sorrow and regret, but her mind was busy. She had to get away and do some thinking, some sorting through her innermost feelings, some mental making sure. She had to dredge up some courage.

She knew it was time to make peace, to mend some hurts before it was too late. It was time to go back and see her mother.

* * *

Sunday, about a month later, was one of those unexpected mid-December days when the sun glistened on the waters of English Bay and its rays tinged the snowcapped peaks of the Lions in golden hues. One of those days when it seemed as if the entire population of Vancouver was out enjoying Stanley Park before the cold and the wet reclaimed its hold on the city.

Isabel, with Kristal in a carrier on her back, was passing HMCS *Discovery* and nearing the end of her walk around the park's perimeter. Slightly winded, she nevertheless maintained her brisk pace while her thoughts dwelled with a mixture of melancholy and satisfaction on the month past.

In many ways the time away from the coffee truck had done her good. It had been a bit of a drain on her savings account, but it was worth it. Away from the seemingly never-ending grind, she'd had a chance to concentrate completely on taking care of Kristal. This had given her the opportunity to really experience what motherhood was all about, and to contemplate its ramifications.

Up until then she'd been too busy meeting the obligations of her coffee route, the challenges of being pregnant and single and the birth of the baby to reflect on what her altered situation really entailed in the long haul.

She had come to the conclusion that, while raising a child alone brought great joy, it could be lonely, as well as hard work. Work that would get harder as the child grew older, became more mobile, developed preferences, demanded to be entertained. Kristal was beginning to do all that, which had made Isabel realize that, if you let it, a child could take up a mother's every waking moment, leaving her no time for a life of her own.

There was the problem, of course. How to create some time and space for yourself without making your child feel neglected. Unwanted. The way she had felt whenever her mother had gone into her studio to paint.

After her father had left that time and never come back, Isabel, then five, had stuck to her mother like a leech. She had crept into her bed at night and followed her everywhere, even into the bathroom. She'd been afraid Delly would leave her, too, and no amount of reasoning or assurance had convinced her otherwise.

Delores's art was the family's sole source of income, however, and so it was imperative that she spend the greater part of each day at work. Alone—after Isabel had ruined several canvases and wreaked general havoc in the studio and on her mother's concentration.

Her grandmother took care of Isabel after that, very lovingly and well, but Isabel had never forgiven her mother for what her childish mind had seen as rejection. She had punished her mother the only way she'd known how, by withholding her love. She'd become a surly child and, later, an unruly, mouthy teenager. Once, she'd sneaked into her mother's studio and destroyed several days' work....

It had been worth being grounded a month to see her mother reduced to tears, but Grandma Abby's sorrow and disappointment in her had hurt. Of course, for that, too, Isabel had blamed her mother, and so it had gone round and round, this spiral of pain in which she and Delores had somehow gotten trapped.

It had taken another loss and even greater pain for Isabel to extricate herself from what had become a hopeless situation. Grandma Abby died of cancer. Delores had known of her mother's illness but, on Abby's express wish, had never told Isabel. As far as the sixteen-year-old Isabel had been concerned, here was the ultimate betrayal. With a final outpouring of grief, resentment and malice, she'd packed a bag and left home.

Throughout the years that followed, searching out her mother's art had been a way of fueling the bitter feelings Isabel harbored toward her. Each painting had been like the twist of a thumbscrew, a searing pain and proof that her mother didn't miss her. Didn't love her. For if she did, how would she have been able to paint such joyful pictures?

Isabel couldn't have said exactly when or how her perceptions had begun to change, nor did it matter. Suffice to say that gradually, as she matured, seeking out her mother's art had ceased to be an act of self-flagellation. It became, instead, a way of making sure Delly was still alive and well.

Just as gradually, Isabel had begun to view the events of her childhood more objectively and had grown to understand some of her mother's needs and difficulties.

In the past month, she and Kristal had stayed in a rented cabin at Ocean Shores, and there, Isabel, too, had taken up painting. While the baby napped, or during sessions in the playpen, she'd experimented with oils and acrylics, and had been able to recharge herself in the process. And she'd come to see what an escape, a release and a solace painting must have been for her mother.

Rather than a rejection of Isabel or merely a way to earn a living, Delores's work in that studio had been a necessary affirmation of her *self*.

Three weeks into her sabbatical, Isabel had finally worked up the courage to go and see her mother. The small house on the fringes of Bellingham, Washington, hadn't changed much—but, oh, what a change its lone occupant had undergone.

When she looked at her own face in the mirror, Isabel thought the thirteen years they'd been apart hadn't left many discernible traces. The same could not be said for Delly, however. On her mother's face the passage of time had carved deep lines. Lines of suffering, but also—incredibly—lines of laughter. Lines that were testimony to the human spirit's amazing capacity to endure.

Amazing, too, had been the lack of constraint between her mother and herself. Considering the circumstances under which Isabel had left home years ago—the bitter recriminations she'd heaped on Delores—she'd been unsure of her welcome. She needn't have been.

When her mother had answered the door and seen her daughter standing there, she had uttered a broken little exclamation and wordlessly opened her arms. They had held each other in silence for long, emotion-charged moments, breaking apart only to drink in each other's features.

Though she had certainly aged, Delores was still unbent. And though the joints in her hands were knotted with arthritis, she had deftly and eagerly taken charge of her grandchild. She had fussed and exclaimed over the baby, hugged her and cried over her, marveled at her perfection.

Later, with Kristal asleep in Isabel's old room, they had talked. Not much, and not that deeply, but it had been good. It had been a start.

Isabel slowed her pace. Almost at her car, she stopped to admire the city's skyline, spectacularly reflected in the waters of Coal Harbour. A man jogged by, and as they all too often had this past month, her thoughts flew to Eric Schwenker. She wondered if he'd missed her and immediately told herself probably not. The baby maybe, but her? After all, the coffee truck had come to his place as usual.

She blinked and sharpened her focus on her powder-blue subcompact car. A tall man was lounging against the hood, his arms and ankles crossed.

Isabel's blood quickened.

As she came closer, intense snapping dark eyes snared hers and didn't let go. "Where the hell have you been all these weeks?"

Eric surprised himself with his sharp tone and imperious phrasing almost as much as he obviously offended Isabel. He hadn't meant to bark like that, hadn't meant to sound quite so belligerent. He watched her stiffen.

"I beg your pardon?"

He wasn't going to be diverted by that icy act of hers, Eric vowed grimly. She had put him through hell disappearing the way she had, and he was going to get some answers.

"I said—"

"I heard you the first time." Lord, he looked good. The black down jacket with chevrons of yellow and royal blue across the chest accentuated the breadth of his torso, while the faded jeans that lovingly hugged the lean strength of his legs sparked longings she'd long since forsworn. Isabel had to fight a sudden urge to run to him, to wrap herself around him—which was why she'd stopped walking and had endeavored to stare him down as coolly as she could.

"Well, then?" His eyes raked her from head to toe. She looked thinner. She looked lovelier. Something hot flared in him.

Unsettled by his scowling perusal, Isabel decided that offense was her best defense. "Just what do you think you're doing here?"

"Waiting for you." He pushed away from the car and began walking toward her. "Looking for you. As, I might add, I've been doing for several weeks now."

"Why, for heaven's sake?" Isabel widened her eyes in mock astonishment.

The question went unanswered, but earned her a glare. "Today one of your neighbors was finally able to tell me where to find you. She also told me the make and color of your car."

His gaze shifted to Kristal, asleep, and softened. He stroked a downy cheek. "She's grown." Then his eyes snapped back to Isabel's. "And she's too heavy for you to carry around any longer. Here, I'll take her."

"You will not." Isabel backed away a step. Her shoulders might be aching, but this take-charge act of his was becoming a definite pain in the neck. "She's my child, in case you've forgotten, and anyway—"

"—you're Wonder Woman, I know."

The barb found its mark. Isabel's breath caught painfully. Was that how she seemed to him? Wonder Woman? Equal to every challenge? She stifled a bitter laugh. If only he knew how tired she was, and how often she felt like a failure....

Well, he obviously didn't know, and he wouldn't hear it from her. "And, anyway," she repeated with a toss of her braid, "Kristal and I are done with our walk."

"Oh." A flush of chagrin tinged Eric's cheeks. He'd overstepped some boundaries, he realized too late. Worrying about her and, yes, dammit, missing her these past several weeks had made him forget that he really had no rights where she was concerned.

He rubbed the back of his neck. "Look, Isabel, I—that is, Frank—was worried sick about you and Kristal when you didn't show up with the truck, so I finally called your house. I left several messages on your machine. When you didn't respond to any of them I went to your place to see what was up. You weren't there."

"I needed to get away." To hide an irrational stab of guilt, Isabel rummaged in her fanny pack for her car keys. "So I took a vacation."

"Without telling anyone?" Her unconcerned attitude exasperated Eric all over again. "Dammit, Isabel—"

Her head snapped up. "I wasn't aware that I owed you an accounting of my plans and whereabouts, *Herr* Schwenker."

"You do when my men count on you to show up, *Ms.* Mott."

"My truck was there as usual."

"Don't change the subject."

"And don't interrogate me," Isabel said angrily. "I'm my own woman. I do as I please, when I please. You got that?"

"Loud and clear." And with that Eric turned and stalked away.

Isabel stared after him with a mixture of fury and guilt. Fury won. Dammit, where did he get off tracking her down like some truant? How dared he demand explanations? The nerve of the man and his macho act. If he thought a few weeks in his spare room entitled him to butt into her life he had another think coming.

Thoroughly upset with him, and with herself, she perched on the edge of the passenger seat of her car and yanked her arms out of the carrier. The procedure of being unstrapped and extracted from the thing woke Kristal up. She started to howl.

"There, there..." She took the baby in her arms, and stood. Crooning, she turned a slow circle while Kristal only cried louder.

"Shh," Isabel soothed, rubbing her back. On top of everything that had just transpired, she wasn't sure she could cope with a crying baby. "Hush, now, please, darling—"

"Here, let me."

Startled by Eric's deep voice behind her, Isabel spun.

"I don't want to fight with you, Isabel." He awkwardly touched his knuckles to her cheek.

"Oh, Eric." She dredged up a wobbly smile.

His lips curved in a smile and he held out his arms. "Why don't you let me hold the little screamer?"

Wordlessly, Isabel handed Kristal over to him. She had experienced a most disturbing jolt at Eric's conciliatory words and gesture. The feeling intensified as she watched him nuzzle the baby's cheek with his nose.

"I've missed you, little love," he whispered tenderly, lifting his eyes to Isabel's as he pressed a kiss on the spot he'd just nuzzled.

Kristal stopped crying, but Isabel felt ridiculously as if she'd like to start.

"Why didn't you tell me you were going to take off for a while?" Eric asked, his voice husky.

"The last time I saw you, I didn't know I was."

"I, that is, we, all of us, didn't know what to think, Isabel. We missed you."

"I'm sorry." She sighed. "I've been on my own for so long I didn't stop to think there might be someone who'd worry. This leave wasn't something I'd planned, it just . . . suddenly seemed necessary."

"What happened?" Scanning her face, Eric thought that for someone who'd just had a month's vacation, Isabel was looking anything but rested. "If you'd care to talk about it . . . ?"

"Oh, I don't know." She wiped a weary hand across her perspiring brow. "It was a lot of things—things I needed to rethink, and things I thought I'd put behind me and no longer mattered. Except I discovered that they did, and that they wouldn't go away until I dealt with them."

Eric shifted Kristal to his other arm and gave her his keys to play with. "Things like what?"

"Relationships. My mother. Among other things on this leave, I went to see her for the first time since I left home at sixteen."

"I see." Eric felt an urge to reach out and touch her again, she looked so vulnerable. But he didn't. She wouldn't want it. He prompted, "And . . . ?"

"Many things. Nothing." She shrugged. "Delly was wonderful, and much more ready to forgive me than it seems I am able to forgive myself. We did some talking, she and I, but thirteen years is a long time."

"Yes." Eric's sigh was empathetic. He could see Isabel was reluctant to elaborate, so he deliberately steered the conversation around to himself. "I haven't seen my mother for many years, either. I'd like to bring her out here for a visit sometime."

"That'd be nice. Is your father alive?"

"Yes, he is."

"You're close?"

Eric shrugged. His father had always been a strong background figure in his life, one he'd heard about almost more than seen. Which was how things were at that time and in that place. His father would go to work during the day, and at night he'd meet and play cards with his cronies. Sometimes he was there for the children to kiss good-night, most times not. All fathers were like that. It was normal.

"I love him," he said simply, and meant it. "How about you? Is your father still living?"

"No." Isabel abruptly looked down at her hands, then more slowly back up at him. "I'm sorry. It's just that the topic of my father..."

"You don't have to explain."

"I know. But thanks." She forced a smile. "Friends again?"

Eric's gaze was warm. "You bet."

The relief Isabel felt was disconcerting. She didn't want to care so much for this man. She cleared her throat. "Thanks, too, for quieting Kristal for me."

"It was my pleasure."

"We should get going."

"Me, too." Neither moved.

"I'm glad you're back, Isabel," Eric finally said, breaking a long pulsing silence between them. And because he felt an almost overwhelming urge to show her how glad with a kiss, he pressed his lips against the forehead of her child. "Shall I put Kristal in the car seat for you?"

"If you like."

"I like."

Almost reluctantly, Isabel stepped aside, but just enough to allow him access to the passenger seat. She inhaled his scent, absorbed his presence and with something like envy watched as he strapped the baby in and kissed her again. She wished—

She caught herself and quickly moved a few steps away.

Eric straightened. "She really is growing," he said. "Maybe you'd better start wheeling her around in one of those buggy contraptions instead of—" Catching her eyes he broke off. His grin was apologetic. "Mind my own business, right?"

"Right." But she said it without heat.

"Goodbye, Isabel." To keep from touching her, Eric stuffed his hands in his pockets and backed away. "I'll see you tomorrow?"

Isabel wordlessly nodded.

Chapter Five

Monday morning brought a return of more seasonal weather and then some. A nasty wind was whipping bare trees into a frenzy and turning umbrellas inside out. Heavy sleet against the truck's windshield had the wipers groaning. In spite of high boots and rain gear, Isabel was wet and chilled to the bone by the time her truck lumbered into the Schwenker parking lot almost an hour behind schedule.

Kristal had been creating her own tempest in the truck's cab off and on all morning. Increasingly fussy, she fidgeted in her car seat, tossed toys to the floor, then cried because they were gone. She didn't want her teething ring, didn't want her bottle. She was quite clearly—and quite understandably, Isabel allowed while praying for patience—fed up with being confined to her seat.

Isabel had no sooner killed the engine when Frank and Eric rushed out of the building. Both men wore such identical expressions of crinkle-faced concern that Isabel had to laugh in spite of her tightly stretched nerves.

"Are you all right?" they shouted in chorus when she stepped from the truck's cab.

"Basically, yes, I suppose." She hurried to unlatch the canopy, her hands not quite steady. "Sorry I'm late."

"Here, I'll do that." Frank said. "You get Kristal inside where it's warm."

"It's warm enough in the truck—"

"Could you please just not argue?" This from Eric who was giving Frank a hand.

Isabel tossed her head, but rounded the hood without another word. She took Kristal out of her seat, tucked her snugly inside her own slicker, grabbed the bag of supplies and jogged toward the office.

"Cripes, what a day." She stepped into the spare room and shook herself like a dog, muttering fiercely beneath her breath. Dropping the bag, she shifted Kristal from arm to arm as she shrugged out of her rain gear.

"Miss," a strident voice reprimanded, "you're dripping water all over this floor."

Isabel's head snapped up. She stared at the elderly woman ensconced behind the desk that had always served as the baby's changing table. "Who're you?"

Behind her, the door opened and closed. Eric walked in, balancing steaming containers of coffee. "Have you ladies met?"

Isabel half turned toward him. "We were just about to, I think."

"Mrs. Jones, this is Isabel Mott, owner-operator of Buns 'n' Java, the truck that brings the morning goodies. Mrs. Jones is our new secretary," he said to Isabel. "She joined the firm two weeks ago."

"I see." Isabel smiled. "Nice to meet you, Mrs. Jones." *I think*, she added silently, noting the woman's tightly pursed lips and the peculiar way her eyes shifted from

Kristal to Eric and back again to Kristal. "Sorry about the drips."

Mrs. Jones muttered something.

"I brought you some coffee." Eric handed one of the cups he was carrying to the dour woman.

"If it's as strong as it was yesterday I can't drink it." She sniffed, then set it down.

"Frank added hot water," said Eric, his voice strained. He turned to Isabel who'd been listening to the exchange with growing astonishment. "Isabel, why don't you and the baby come into my office. I've moved the sofa in there."

"Where on earth did you get *her?*" Isabel asked as soon as the door shut behind them.

Eric looked to be in pain as he rounded his desk and sat down. "She was the first applicant the employment agency sent me."

"So?"

"So she had a whole stack of references and all the office skills I required." He shrugged uncomfortably. "I couldn't think of a plausible reason not to hire her."

Isabel was already unwrapping a happily gurgling Kristal with efficient dispatch. At Eric's somewhat halting reply, she slanted him a sharp glance. "Do you like her?"

"Well, I..." Eric slumped back in his chair. The fact was that, aside from her unpleasantness, he found the woman intolerable to work with. She disregarded most of his requests and suggestions and did things exactly when and how she chose, *if* she chose. She was surly to him and his customers and ignored Frank LeFleur and his men altogether. So, did he like her?

"No. But she's no longer young and—" He broke off, and with a sigh, wearily pinched the bridge of his nose.

"To be perfectly honest, I don't know *what* to do about her."

Isabel closed the last snap on Kristal's romper with a decisive click. "You realize, of course, that you should never have hired the first person who applied."

"But she was qualified—"

"That's not the point."

"And she seemed to expect—"

"Aha!" Isabel picked up her child and turned to face Eric. "Just as I thought. You let her bully you into it, didn't you?"

Eric's expression turned sheepish. "Sort of, I suppose." At Isabel's incredulous laugh, he flushed. "Well, dammit, Isabel, you've seen her," he blustered. "She's not a woman who's easily dismissed—"

"*I'd* have had no trouble dismissing her."

"Oh, really?"

"Really!"

"All right, then." He rose so abruptly, his chair slammed into the wall behind him. "Give me the child and let's see you do it."

For an instant Isabel didn't move. She hadn't expected him to take her boast seriously. Seeing he did, she handed Kristal to him.

"Fine. No problem." She marched from the room as if into battle.

Mrs. Jones was lounging back in her chair, having a whispered conversation on the phone that didn't sound like business to Isabel as she stopped in front of the desk. The woman glared up at her. When Isabel continued to stand there, she said, "Hold it, Muriel," and pressed the receiver against an ample shoulder. "Yes?"

Isabel smiled coolly. "I'd like a word with you, Mrs. Jones. When you've got a moment," she added after a pointed pause.

Mrs. Jones frowned her displeasure and made a clacking sound with her tongue as she heaved a put-upon sigh. "Call you right back," she told Muriel, slowly straightening to hang up the phone. "Yes?" she inquired again, sharply.

"You're fired, Mrs. Jones," Isabel told her with icy courtesy.

The woman's mouth dropped open. "*You* can't fire me."

"I just did."

"Mr. Schwenker—"

"—is otherwise occupied at the moment. Your check and two weeks' severance pay will be in the mail by tonight. If I were you, I'd take the money and run."

"Harrumph." Mrs. Jones surged to her feet. "The agency—"

"—will be notified of your conduct should you choose to become difficult." Isabel moved swiftly around the desk and tugged three notepads out of the woman's open purse. The Schwenker Engineering logo was prominent on each of them. "I don't think your record could stand another blotch, do you?"

Mrs. Jones looked Isabel up and down with a malevolent sneer. "Men are fools," she hissed. "And that one more so than most for taking up with the likes of you."

"Goodbye," Isabel said coldly. She stayed where she was until the woman had left. Afterward, back in Eric's office, she snatched Kristal off his lap.

"Done," she snapped, smarting from the woman's parting shot though she knew she shouldn't, and irrationally taking it out on Eric. "So. Do you have a micro-wave?"

"What?" Eric found it difficult to shift mental gears as rapidly as Isabel apparently could.

"A microwave. To warm Kristal's bottle." She bent to pull it from the bag. "I'm in here to feed my child, you know, not solve your personnel problems."

"Bottle?" Eric didn't hear the rest. "Whatever happened to..." He faltered, cleared his throat. "I mean..."

"Dried up." Isabel straightened and, seeing his flushed face, couldn't help but laugh. "You have a puritanical streak a mile wide. Aren't you the one who called breast-feeding the most natural of acts?"

"Well, I..."

That was generic, he wanted to say. *This is you.* Though he'd be damned if he cared to examine why that made a difference. Best just to drop it. "Anyway, there's no microwave." He frowned. "Is that a problem?"

"A slight glitch, that's all. I'll get some hot water from the truck and warm the bottle in that."

"I'll get it for you." He rose, but then stood irresolute. "So what happened with Mrs. Jones?"

"She's gone."

"Just like that?"

"Yup." At his frown, Isabel suddenly realized just how irrational her behavior must look to him. "I'm sorry," she said, coming to stand in front of his desk. "That woman upset me. You know she was a thief on top of everything else? I wish I'd known that before I offered her two weeks' severance pay."

"A thief?" What was there for the woman to steal in *this* office?

Isabel answered his unvoiced question. "Supplies," she said. "Pens, pencils, stuff like that. She had three notepads with your logo sticking out of her purse."

"Oh, for crying out loud." Eric rubbed the back of his neck. "And here I thought a secretary would solve some of my problems, not add to them. Now what?"

"Now you get someone else," Isabel said glibly. "But first, you'd better get me that hot water you promised."

"Right." On his way out, Eric wondered if he shouldn't put Frank in charge of this secretary thing. Frank always handled the hiring and firing in the shop, so why not for the office? Dealing with people on that kind of level just wasn't Eric's forte. He was an engineer; he knew about machines and formulas, logical matters. There was no logic when it came to people. Witness his dealings with Isabel Mott. He still hadn't figured out what it was that drew him to her so relentlessly when she wasn't even remotely his type.

After Eric left, Isabel put Kristal down on the carpeted floor. "You were a whole lot less trouble when you were littler, funny face," she murmured, handing her a chewy toy. These days the kid chewed on everything. "We're going to have to come up with a plan 'B' of sorts here...."

"Hey, look who's sitting up by herself!" Eric exclaimed, coming back with the container of hot water. "I can't believe it."

"Believe it." Isabel massaged the small of her back as she straightened. She plunged the bottle into the water with a rueful shake of her head. "Wouldn't you know, *here* she likes to sit, but in the truck, forget it. This young lady got a taste of freedom these past few weeks and she's not about to give it up gracefully."

Plucking the bottle out of its bath, she shook it, tested its temperature and stuck it back in. "I guess she'll adjust in a day or so. Don't you think?" she prompted Eric.

Unhappy with the situation but at a loss as to how to make it better, she was hoping some input from an uninvolved party might help.

"Hmm," Eric said, brows furrowed.

Isabel eyed him askance, muttering, "You're such a help, R.E." Plunking herself down on the floor, she lifted Kristal onto her lap with a grunt.

"Hmm?" Eric said again, absently. Catching Isabel's wry glance, he colored. "Sorry. I was thinking..."

"Really?"

"There's no need for sarcasm, Ms. Mott." He lowered himself to the floor next to them. "As it happens I was thinking about you. The two of you," he quickly added when her eyes narrowed. "I've got a proposition to make you that I think we'll both be happy with."

"Proposition, huh? This better not be—"

"Ms. Mott!" Eric interrupted with pretended shock. He tut-tutted, but was obviously pleased with himself. "You forget there is a *Mrs.* Schwenker—"

"You mean your mother?"

Eric's brows shot upward. "Who told you?"

"Frank."

"The man's history."

"No, he's not. You'd go broke in a month. Here, drink some more, sweetie." Isabel teased the baby's lips with the rubber nipple, then grinned up at Eric as Kristal latched onto her bottle. "So why did you want me to think you were married?"

Eric took a moment to inspect the fingernails on his left hand, then lifted twinkling eyes to hers. "You seemed to expect me to be."

Their gazes tangled. Heat instantly kindled in Isabel's chest. She quickly glanced down at Kristal and gave a self-conscious laugh. "Yeah. I remember."

Foolishly relieved because it seemed Eric hadn't made up a wife in order to keep her at arm's length, after all, she chuckled. "I used to picture your wife as some apple-cheeked dumpling of a hausfrau in an apron."

"You did?" He laughed, too. "Actually, that's Frau Schultz, my housekeeper, you've just described. I'm very fond of her."

"I'll bet you are." In control of her reactions again, Isabel gave him a pointed look. "And I bet she waits on you hand and foot."

"Pretty much, yes." He bristled when Isabel made a derisive sound. "What's wrong with that? She's doing woman's work in a nice home for good pay—"

"*Woman's* work?" Isabel hooted. "I don't believe this! Woman's work." She rolled her eyes. "You mean she cooks, cleans, et cetera, et cetera. Right?"

"Right." He watched her eyes narrow. "What are you getting so hot about?"

"I'm getting hot, as you put it, because if your Frau Schultz is doing woman's work, what the hell do you think I'm doing, huh?"

"Feeding Kristal—"

"I don't mean feeding Kristal and you know it, R. E. Schwenker! Running my business, driving my truck, all the other jobs I've done in my time is what I mean. Man's work to you, I suppose?"

"Well . . ."

She stuck her nose close to his face. "Is it?"

"Well, yes, when you get right down to it."

"I knew it!" Isabel drew back, triumphant. "And I'll just bet the proposition you have for me has to do with more suitable—as in woman's—work, doesn't it?"

"Well, yes," he repeated, thinking she certainly had a knack for making a big to-do about nothing. "As a matter of fact, it does. If you can type, that is."

"Well, of course I can type, but—"

"Great! Can you file? Keep books? Answer the phone?"

"Certainly, but—"

"All right, then, there you are."

"I am?"

"Yup." Lithely, he got to his feet and beamed down at her. "Ms. Mott, I'm hiring you as the new secretary. You can bring Kristal with you to work every day."

"Well, well, well." Isabel carefully lifted Kristal to her shoulder and made a production out of rubbing the baby's back. "You have been busy thinking, haven't you?"

She patted her daughter's back some more, then looked at Eric with narrowed eyes. "Why?"

At that, Eric's smile fled. Dammit, he'd made the offer in good faith. Did she have to be so infuriatingly suspicious all the time? "Do you want the job or not?"

"Well..." Isabel knew it was the perfect solution, but darn it, he was such a chauvinist. Accepting it would put her deeper into his debt, too, wouldn't it? Yet where else would she get such an opportunity? And working with Eric, being around him all day, every day...

She coolly met his scowl. "I'll think about it."

"Don't do me any favors." God, the woman was stiff-necked and irritating.

"I don't plan to."

They glared at each other. At length Eric snapped, "Well?"

Isabel stuck out her chin. "I've thought about it."

"And?"

"What's the salary?"

Teeth clenched, Eric named a generous sum.

Isabel tried not to blink an eye as she forced an unimpressed shrug. "Benefits?"

That did it. "Dammit, a heated office and a roof over your head."

Isabel smiled. Chalk one up for her side, she congratulated herself. She'd show him woman's work. The man belonged with the dinosaurs.

Setting Kristal down on the rug, she gave him a cool glance. "I'll take it."

Eric expelled a hard breath and contemplated her smug expression with a slow shake of the head. "Whatever made me think Mrs. Jones was bad?"

Isabel's shrug had been intended to seem facetiously innocent, but her gaze got tangled up with his and intentions evaporated like fog in the sun. Studying each other, neither smiled anymore. Isabel willed her suddenly galloping pulse back to normal. When it wouldn't obey, she wrenched her eyes from his and cleared her throat.

"You, uh, you've done it again, you know."

"Done what?" Eric asked huskily. When she neither responded nor looked up at him, he squatted down and gently tilted her chin with one finger. "Done what?"

Isabel's mouth went dry. He was so near, and his eyes were so dark. She nervously cleared her throat again. "Hired someone without looking around. What if I don't work out?"

"You will." Eric could feel her pulse thrumming against his finger. His own heartbeat accelerated to match hers. Of their own accord his other fingers spread against the delicate curve of Isabel's jaw. "Things'll work out just fine."

"I wouldn't be too sure."

"I would."

Their gazes seemed to fuse as something hot and electrifying arced between them.

"Why?" Isabel breathed, no longer sure just what they were discussing. Worse, she no longer cared.

"Because," he whispered.

Isabel's gaze dropped to his mouth, traced its finely etched lines, watched his lips shape the word. Suddenly, she had an overwhelming desire to feel those lips against her own. To taste them, to experience their texture. Would they feel as warm as the breath that whispered across them toward her? Would they be as soft, yet unyielding, as they looked? She longed to know, and she moved, ever so fractionally, toward finding out.

To hell with it, Eric thought, watching her lids flutter, feeling the sigh that trembled across her lips and mingled with his own. *I'm going to kiss her.*

As if drawn by a magnet, he bent toward her, lowered his mouth to hers. He moistened and parted his lips just as she was doing. His eyelids drooped—

The phone shrilled.

Isabel gasped; her eyes flew open. She jerked back, then scrambled to her feet.

Temptation had passed. Letting his chin drop to his chest with an explosive sigh, Eric told himself it was best this way. But, somehow, he couldn't quite believe it.

Isabel could. Oh, yes, indeed. Saved by the bell, and then some. She must have been mad. What could she have been thinking? And what was she doing, taking a job in this man's office?

She didn't need for the windshield wipers to be stuck again, gummed up with wet snow, to know the answer.

Anything was better than being out driving in this weather or, for that matter, serving up coffee and snacks with a howling child. There were other jobs, of course. She'd never had trouble finding employment before and she wouldn't now. She was still in good shape, she could go back to teaching aerobics classes with Kristal at her feet.

But the pay was lousy.

Well, then—she still knew all the recipes and could learn whatever novelty drinks were in vogue now. She could go back to tending bar.

But those smoke-filled taverns... Isabel wrinkled her nose. Her lungs were just beginning to recuperate. And what about Kristal?

She could go back to slinging hash, and smell like deep-fried fish and overheated oil all the time. Besides, there, too, what about Kristal?

Selling real estate hadn't been bad, nor had cashiering, clerking, or parking cars. But... what about Kristal?

Day care.

The light ahead changed to red. Isabel slammed on the brake, skidded, fought for control of her vehicle. Horns blared as she narrowly avoided several collisions. Infuriated drivers glared and mouthed blessedly unheard obscenities. Isabel's hands and knees trembled.

Day care was out of the question.

She carefully accelerated and drove on toward home. Walking into the warmth of her living room with her little girl, now asleep, bundled in her arms, Isabel knew that she would do *anything* to avoid having strangers raise her child. Never mind that the cost of decent day care was prohibitive in terms of dollars and cents, the cost in terms of lost time and intimacy was ever so much greater.

And so there remained R. E. Schwenker and his proposition. The welfare of her child demanded she accept and live with it.

Isabel gently laid Kristal in her crib. She unzipped but didn't remove the child's quilted outer garment and tiptoed from the room. As she did, she resolved that from now on emotions would not be allowed any part in her dealings with Eric Schwenker, nor would they be allowed to interfere with the job she'd been hired to do. The brief moments of tension and attraction they'd shared that morning had been brought on by the stresses and strains that had preceded them. They would not be repeated. It was as simple as that.

Feeling much better about everything, Isabel peeled off her clothes, letting them drop to the floor as she headed for a warming shower. Afterward, cozy in a black velour jumpsuit and fuzzy slippers, she drifted into the kitchen, put the kettle on to boil and rummaged in her cupboard for a clean mug. Not able to find one, she sorted through the sinkful of dishes, then rinsed out the first one she unearthed. Later she'd better get the dishwasher loaded; she was running low on baby bottles, too.

She pulled a face and, waiting for the water to heat for her tea, flipped on the message switch of her answering machine. Listening absently to a reminder from her dentist, then to the beep and hum of someone who'd hung up without speaking, she located a bag of mint tea. The last message, however, had her paying attention. It was her mother.

"Is everything all right, child?" Delly was saying. "I haven't heard from you since I saw you ten days ago. Please call."

Thoughtful, her movements slow, Isabel switched off the machine, then turned to pour water over her tea bag.

Delly had sounded worried. Unbidden, the old resentments bubbled up, and she thought, *For thirteen years she's been content to let me be what and where I chose, and now she worries. She has no right. One visit doesn't entitle her...*

Stop it, a sane inner voice inside Isabel chided. Somewhat shamefaced, she forced her thoughts away from past hurts, real or imagined. She had promised herself to let go of all that, to only look forward. Nobody said it'd be easy.

She carried her hot drink into the living room and picked up the phone. Her finger stabbed out her mother's number automatically. She knew it by heart, had never forgotten it, though this was the first call home she'd made in more than thirteen years.

The third ring produced a reply. "Hello."

It was a man's voice, deep, gruff. Isabel frowned, almost hung up. Who on earth...?

"Delores Kant, please."

"Who's this?" The voice remained uncordial.

Isabel bristled. "I might ask you the same thing," she countered. "I'm—"

"The prodigal daughter," the man interrupted with a chuckle warming his voice. "I got you now. Hold on a minute."

Frowning, Isabel listened to a brief muffled exchange and then her mother's still surprisingly young voice said, "Hello, dear. Thank you for returning my call."

"Who was that man?" Isabel demanded, and was instantly chagrined. Good Lord, she thought, if Delly asked me a question like that I'd spit nails. "I'm sorry, I—"

"It's all right." Her mother's small laugh ended in a fit of coughing. "It's Doc Kramer. You remember him."

Doc Kramer. The picture of an immense hulk of a man with the beard and smile of a young Santa Claus projected itself into Isabel's mental screen. He'd been the family doctor for as long as she could remember.

"I've got this nasty cough that won't let go," her mother went on to explain. "Marcus stopped by to check up on me, and also to prescribe more of his nasty concoctions for my hands."

Delly was ill. Guilt settled like a mantle on Isabel's shoulders. "I'm sorry I didn't call you sooner."

"It's all right," her mother soothed. "I've got a cold, that's all."

"I've had a lot to think about," Isabel felt compelled to elaborate defensively. "A lot of things to digest and lots of feelings to sort out since I saw you . . ."

"Of course you have. I understand, dear, perfectly. Please, I didn't mean to rush you into anything. I...I was noticing the weather, and I thought of you driving around in it. I was worried, that's all."

Isabel could hear it in her voice. Love, longing and concern. It brought a lump to her throat. She forced it down, but couldn't quite suppress another urge of resentment. "I learned long ago how to look after myself, Mother."

"I know. And I'm sorry."

The quietness of her mother's reply affected Isabel much more than a screeching rebuke would have. Her head dropped. Why was she doing this to both of them? Had she returned her mother's call merely to make them both miserable?

"I'm sorry, too. Look, Mom—" the name she hadn't used since long before she'd even left home fell from her tongue with unexpected ease "—it may not sound like it, but I'd like us to have a relationship like other mothers and daughters. . . ."

Her mother's soft rueful chuckle caused her to pause.

"What?" Isabel asked.

"Child, I'm afraid that's pretty much what we've *been* having all these years," Delores said sadly. "I'm afraid we women, all of us to varying degrees, are genetically programmed to chafe at the ties that bind us to our mothers. The sad thing is, many of us never manage to move beyond the mother-daughter struggle to friendship."

"But you and Grandma Abby..."

"Had to overcome all manner of problems before our love and respect for each other allowed us to be who we were. And even then, given the circumstances of my marriage and the problems you and I were having, it was often difficult."

She paused, audibly swallowed, then coughed. "Darn virus," she said hoarsely when she could speak again.

"Isabel, we three—you, me and Kristal—are all the family each of us has left in the world. I know you won't believe this now, but the day will come when your daughter, too, will rattle the cage of your love for her and demand to be free of you. You'll never stop loving her, but you'll have to let her go. Just as I had to let you go, darling. With luck she'll come back to you sooner than you did to me. How do you think you'll feel then?"

How would she feel? Isabel squeezed her eyes shut against a rush of tears. She'd be heartbroken if Kristal rejected her, and ecstatic when she returned.

"You see?" her mother said softly, as if she'd read Isabel's thoughts. "Now do you see?"

Isabel nodded, her eyes still tightly closed. She realized Delly had no way of perceiving her nod and managed a choked "Yes."

They said little more that afternoon. It had all been said, hadn't it? And while the reality of their newfound understanding and acceptance of each other might take time to solidify, neither of them doubted that solidify it would.

"It'll be Christmas in just two weeks," Isabel said in closing. "Will you come spend it with us?"

When her mother replied that she would, Isabel felt as if she had just received the very best present ever.

Suddenly the holidays ahead no longer loomed, but beckoned. She had dreaded them, having been all too familiar with the loneliness that stole the joy and replaced it with envy if a person weren't careful. In years past, before her marriage, before Kristal, she'd always made it a point to spend Christmas Eve and Christmas Day at the shelters for the homeless of whatever city she happened to be living in at the time. There she would help with the cooking and serving of meals to those even more lonely and forgotten than she, and that had helped.

Less unencumbered now that she had a small child, Isabel had nevertheless planned to at least deliver a box of presents and groceries to one of the missions. She decided she still would; Delly would love it.

Isabel stopped in the act of getting up from her chair as a long-buried memory chose that moment to surface. A memory of herself, maybe seven or eight years old. And of Delores, tall and blond. Beautiful. They were hand in hand, standing in front of a weather-beaten door, singing carols. They each carried a basket. Isabel's held gaily wrapped presents, things both Delly and Grandma Abby had made. Knitted gloves and stocking caps; jams and preserves; homemade cookies. Her mother's basket had been heavy with the makings of a Christmas dinner.

Isabel remembered that their own gifts to each other had been no more elaborate, and their holiday meal sometimes less so. She could see again the smiling look her mother and grandmother exchanged as they told her, "The joy is in the giving."

And so it was. Settling back in her chair, she picked up the knitting project she had started a few days ago and eyed it with satisfaction. She imagined Eric's pleasure and surprise when she presented him with this token of her appreciation. She could see his smile, and felt a glow of anticipation.

Chapter Six

"All right, along that wall will be fine. A little more to the left... Right. Great. Thanks, Frank."

Isabel eyed the pair of new metal filing cabinets with approval, then turned to Eric who stood loaded down with stacks of manila file folders. Rolled-up technical drawings stuck out from under his arms like crazy antennae.

On the floor behind him, Kristal peeked wide-eyed over the top of the cardboard box in which she sat.

"You can put those on the floor in front of the cabinets, please," Isabel directed her new boss. She'd been on the job as Schwenker Engineering's secretary for three days. So far she'd done little typing, filing or keeping of books. "And then bring the rest of the stuff from your office. I'll put order into this mess you laughingly call a filing system if it's the last thing I do."

"I've always managed to find what I needed," Eric grumbled around the sheet of foolscap he held clamped between his teeth.

Isabel ignored his rejoinder and relieved him of the paper. "What's this?"

"The list of names you wanted." He bent to set down his burdens.

"Ah, yes. The people it's okay to interrupt you for." Isabel scanned the list and her eyes snapped to his. "These are all women."

"Right." Straightening, he shrugged modestly and stifled a grin. No need to tell Isabel he'd scoured his little black book for names just to get a rise out of her. She had such a poor opinion of men, was always thinking the worst of them. More than once she'd implied that he, Eric, must surely be a regular Casanova. God knew where she'd gotten that impression. Though he did have numerous female acquaintances—casual dates, and every one of them on Isabel's list—he tended to be reticent about forming romantic attachments. He had yet to meet the woman with whom he'd like to share his life, a woman he could love and take care of, a woman who would love and pamper him in return.

A woman like—his gaze collided with Isabel's, and he completed the thought with a sense of shock—*Isabel Mott?*

No, no. He quickly dismissed the thought, remembering that he'd been over that with himself. The woman of his dreams was only a *little* like Isabel, that was all. She might be fine-boned, yet womanly like her; someone as outwardly delicate, yet inwardly strong; maybe she'd have Isabel's wit and courage and, yes, her warmth—though Isabel generally chose to display that warmth only for Kristal, didn't she?

Eric's lips tightened as an unpleasant sensation curled in his stomach. And for Frank. But for him she seemed to feel nothing beyond casual friendship. Which was good,

Eric hastened to assure himself, since he certainly felt
nothing more for her. Heaven forbid.

The woman was way too independent, even aggressive,
for his taste. She didn't seem to need anyone, least of all
him, and would neither want nor welcome the kind of love
and care he had it in him to give. As for her being the kind
of wife and mother he envisioned for himself and his children—ha! He'd laugh, if he weren't suddenly so ticked off.

"Names will likely be added or deleted from time to
time," he said. Who was she to eye him so judgmentally?

"I'm sure." Isabel replied, the expression in her eyes as
cool as peppermint. She'd be damned if she'd let him see
that his stupid list upset her.

"Any problems with that?"

"Problems?" She slapped the paper down on her desk.
"None at all." She strode to the new file cabinets. Yank-
ing open a drawer, she snapped, "I don't know about you,
but I've got work to do."

"So do I." Eric turned away. "Thanks to you, I'm days
behind."

For three days he and Frank had been toting and cart-
ing for the woman like a couple of coolies. He glanced at
his foreman.

Frank stood thoughtfully scratching his scalp beneath a
lifted cap, while listening to their exchange with avid and
undisguised interest.

Great! Eric let out a puff of air and massaged the back
of his neck. He'd forgotten about Frank. He wondered
about the man's thoughts but couldn't decipher his expression.

"There's one more crate of drawings in my office," he
said to Frank, rather more curtly than he usually spoke to
his men. "Let's drag it out here, shall we, so the two of us
can get on with the work we're supposed to do."

Frank quickly dropped his cap in place, and stepped around Kristal and into Eric's office. Eric stayed behind for one more duel of glances with Isabel.

"I trust you can manage on your own after this, Ms. Mott?"

"Certainly, Herr Schwenker." Her lips thinned. "If you were too busy to move things for me you should've said so. I could have gotten someone else from the shop."

"That's all I'd have needed—" Eric disgustedly turned to follow Frank "—the union on my back because one of their members is doing work he wasn't hired to do."

He stopped at Kristal's box. Bending to retrieve the toys she'd tossed out, he sniffed. "Don't you ever change this child?" He lifted the little girl out of her makeshift playpen. "Or am I expected to do that, too?"

"Well!" In a flash of red-faced indignation Isabel was in front of him. She snatched her daughter out of his gentle hold and stormed out to the rest room where Eric had managed to rig up a changing station of sorts.

The door slammed shut behind her, and Eric frowned. Damn the woman and the crazy mixture of emotions she never failed to stir up in him. He'd been an idiot, asking her to come and work for him. He didn't need the distraction of her, the aggravation of her. Life had been quiet and orderly before she'd come into it, and he'd liked it that way.

Now he rarely had a moment of peace, of uninterrupted work; she was always *there,* even if physically she wasn't. At those times when he sat at his desk and she at hers, and the door between their offices was closed, she still interfered with his thoughts. He sensed her, heard her, even thought he could feel and smell her. She had this scent, a combination of baby smells and perfume, which always made him long to gather her close and bury his nose in the soft warmth of her neck.

Of course, he'd never actually *do* such a thing. But he wanted to, and that irked him. He'd have liked to be able to blame her, but couldn't. She never acted in any way provocatively toward him. Quite the contrary. She was as prickly, as stiff-necked and opinionated as ever with him.

She looked different, however. Gone were the down vests, the men's shirts, the jeans. In their place she wore smart slacks or graceful skirts, which emphasized the slim lines of her long legs and gently rounded derriere. And sweaters, which made no secret of breasts still high and shapely in spite of motherhood. Her hair was different, too. Softer now, caught loosely at the nape of her neck or gathered on top of her head with combs and such. It looked shiny, rich and lustrous, and more than once he'd itched to bury his hands in it.

They were ridiculous, these wants and feelings that kept creeping up on him, and, given their employer-employee relationship, they were entirely inappropriate. It was crucial for him to keep his distance, to maintain no more than a friendly *working* relationship with Isabel Mott. It was what she wanted, in any case. And of course it was what he wanted, too.

Turning with an audible sigh, he found himself once again the object of Frank LeFleur's speculative scrutiny. The men regarded each other in solemn silence for a moment.

"Things'll never be the same, boss," Frank predicted.

Amen, Eric thought grimly.

A few days later, Isabel had her new life and office organized and running like a well-oiled clock. The coffee truck had been leased out to the same woman who had substituted for Isabel during her impromptu vacation. It still stopped daily at Schwenker, though Frank no longer played host. Isabel had decided not to sell the business outright just yet; she needed the security of knowing it was there to fall back on should this secretarial job not work out for her.

And it might well not. R. E. Schwenker had turned into a real bear these past few days, speaking to her as if they were strangers and keeping his distance even from Kristal. Isabel told herself it didn't matter. He was a man, after all, and she'd learned not to trust men. With R.E. she'd been close to forgetting those hard-learned lessons, for he'd always been so mild-tempered and nice.

Hadn't Arnie Mott been, too, in the beginning? And look how cruelly he had betrayed the trust she'd been foolish enough to place in him. She ought to be thankful that R. E. Schwenker was showing his true colors this early.

Last night she had unraveled the sweater she'd begun to knit him for Christmas, deciding the gift was too personal. The holiday was three days away; she'd buy him some impersonal token—a pen-and-pencil set or some such—to show she appreciated the job he'd given her. After all, it did allow her to have her daughter right here within reach, and for now, at least, that was important. Later... well, she'd see.

Kristal spit out the nipple for the third time, and Isabel finally got the message that the child was full. She'd been too preoccupied to notice, thinking as she had about how she hated the part of her job that required her to deal with Eric's personal calls.

She despised herself for instantly disliking any female who asked for Eric—no, Rudy. None of them ever asked to speak to Eric, not even that Marcia....

Isabel resolutely banished the name, and the sultry voice that went along with it, from her mind. Kristal was done eating, and it was time for her nap. Isabel carried her into Eric's office and laid her down in the playpen, which served as her daytime bed. Eric had breezed out of the office earlier, in a much happier mood than he'd been in for days. In fact, he'd looked like a little boy with a secret, and he wouldn't tell her where he was going. Maybe he had a date....

There she went again! As if a man as dedicated to his business as Eric would go off on a date in the middle of the workday!

Fed up with herself, Isabel shook off her ruminations and peeked once more at her sleeping daughter. Besides, what R.E. did with his time was none of her business. She tiptoed out, closing the door with care just as the one across her office swung wide. Turning, Isabel saw a redhead in a full-length silver mink glide in on a cloud of expensive perfume. Something told her this was no customer wanting to purchase a crane.

"May I help you?" Isabel took pride in the fact that she managed to maintain her professional courtesy in spite of the unpleasant flutters in her stomach. She just knew this was one of *them*.

"Yes," the woman said in a soft voice. "I'd like to see Mr. Schwenker, please. I'm Marcia Butler."

Marcia Butler in the flesh was even more unnerving than her sultry voice over the phone had been.

The clutch in Isabel's stomach intensified. Slowly, with a sinking heart, she scanned the elegant length of the woman whose name topped the list Eric had given her. She was stunning.

Or would be, Isabel amended, recalling her principles, if she didn't have the bad taste to drape herself in the skins of dead animals. Isabel's strong feelings on the matter helped considerably in ignoring the woman's open and friendly smile.

She walked to her desk and sat down. "Mr. Schwenker is out."

"Oh?" Marcia's face mirrored the disappointment in her voice. She lifted an exquisitely wrapped little parcel. "I told him I'd be by with his Christmas present this morning."

"He must have forgotten." Isabel assessed the small box in the kid-gloved hand. It contained something with a designer label, no doubt. Something expensive. Something that would have made the sweater she'd been knitting seem decidedly tacky. Good thing she'd undone it.

"If you'd like to leave the gift," she suggested curtly, "I'll see he gets it."

"Well…" Marcia looked undecided. She glanced at her watch, minuscule and sparkling with diamonds. "I *am* on my way to the airport…"

Goody, thought Isabel.

"…and I won't be back until after New Year's…"

Even better. Isabel allowed a thin smile to blossom.

"…so I guess it *would* be best if I left it—"

"Ho, ho, ho!"

Isabel jumped to her feet and Marcia spun around at the sound of the male voice ho-hoing from behind a potted fir tree.

"Merry Christmas!" it boomed.

"Rudy!" exclaimed Marcia delightedly as Eric struggled through the door with the tree.

"Shh!" Isabel admonished. "The baby's asleep."

"I was afraid I'd missed you, darling," Marcia caroled, undaunted.

"Shh!" Isabel and Eric hissed in unison.

"What baby?" Marcia demanded.

"Ours. I mean, hers," Eric absently corrected, closing the door with his foot as he set down the tree. "Isabel's." He straightened. "Is she in my office?"

"'Fraid so." Isabel shrugged. "Of course I had no idea you were expecting a visitor. Shall I move Kristal?"

"Don't be silly." Eric turned to Marcia. "Forgive us, won't you? When it comes to that child we tend to be overprotective." He clasped her shoulders. "You look lovely," he said sincerely.

He liked Marcia very much; she was sweet-natured and fun to be with. Besides which, any man would be proud to be seen with her. For the past five months he'd quite happily been the only man who'd had the privilege of escorting her, but just lately he'd gone out of his way to avoid her. It was over between them, he could now admit.

His gaze flew to Isabel. Was it the light, or were her eyes greener than usual? It seemed to him they glittered like shards of emeralds before she quickly veiled them with her lashes and looked down.

She was upset about something and it had to do with him, Eric was sure of it. Feeling oddly guilty to be holding Marcia, he released her and stepped back a pace. He cleared a suddenly scratchy throat.

"So. Have you ladies met?"

Isabel didn't answer.

Marcia's reply was a question. "Why is your secretary's child sleeping in your office?" Her speculative glance shot from Eric to Isabel and back to Eric. "Is it ill?"

"No, *she's* not ill," Isabel said frostily before Eric could reply. "Kristal always takes her naps there."

"Kristal does?" Marcia turned to Eric. "Rudy, is this true?"

"Um, yes. Yes, it is." Discomfited by what was clearly becoming an inexplicably hostile situation, he stuck his hands in his pockets and hunched his shoulders. There were vibrations in the air here that were strong enough to make his ears hum.

"Isn't that a bit . . . unorthodox?" Marcia queried.

"I . . ." At a loss, Eric shrugged. Having Kristal sleep in his office had seemed like a logical solution to him. After all, it was quietest there. On the other hand, he was no expert on child-rearing. Maybe it was unorthodox. He turned to Isabel. "Is it?"

"I don't know." Isabel shrugged, too, though she wasn't as bewildered by Marcia's attitude as Eric was. She was a woman, after all, and could recognize feminine jealousy when she saw it—even if she couldn't admit to feeling it herself. What she couldn't understand was what Marcia thought she had to worry about. So a child slept in her lover's office. So what?

Isabel gave another shrug. "I can only say that so far the arrangement has worked for us. When Kristal sleeps, I hold Eric's calls and, consequently, he's able to get most of his design work done during that time."

"Eric?" Marcia's carefully shaped eyebrows snapped together. "Who on earth is Eric?"

Isabel merely looked at him.

He could feel a flush coming on and wished himself in Timbuktu. Why did he feel like the bone two dogs were fighting over?

"I am," he said, pricked by Marcia's piercing stare as by so many needles. How had a perfectly harmless working relationship between himself and Isabel become so difficult to explain?

He cleared his throat again. "It's what my family calls me."

"This woman is part of your family?"

Eric's and Isabel's gazes met. Dipping deeply, he saw that hers was expectant. And something else...

"In a manner of speaking," he allowed, keeping his eyes on Isabel's and trying to decipher what that "something else" could be. Disillusionment? Hope? A little of both? Whatever it was, it tugged at his heartstrings. He gave her a smile.

"Isabel is a good friend," he said, still holding her gaze. "And I care very much for her child."

The warmth of Eric's gaze, as well as his words, made Isabel's heart contract and then expand. Something shifted forcefully inside her, much as glacial ice shifts when it starts to melt. Her gaze on his warmed; the smile she offered him turned her eyes into luminous stars.

"I see." Marcia's voice, and the edge it contained, brought Isabel and Eric abruptly out of their mutual contemplation.

Eric turned to Marcia. "I think you misunderstand—"

"On the contrary." She tossed her head and drew her coat tightly around herself. She studied him coolly, and at length. As she did, gradually, the frost in her eyes melted. Shaking her head with a little laugh, she stepped close and framed his face with her hands. "It's you who doesn't understand, Rudy," she murmured. "Not yet, anyway."

Before he could react, and much to Isabel's outrage, she kissed him full on the mouth. "It's been grand, darling," she whispered. "Be happy."

She exited in a swirl of silk and fur, leaving Isabel and Eric to stare first at the door, then again, briefly, at each other.

And then Eric was hurrying out the door, too.

Drained suddenly, Isabel collapsed into the chair. She propped her elbows on the desk and wearily let her face drop into her hands.

What had happened just then? she wondered dismally. And what was happening now, outside? Depression settled on her like a winter fog. She shivered, well able to imagine the scene as Eric undoubtedly tried to mend fences with the beautiful Marcia.

"Isabel?"

She snapped erect. Her eyes met Eric's concerned ones.

"What's wrong?" He reached out to touch her forehead. "A headache?"

She jerked away from his touch, but then, feeling foolish, sighed and nodded. "Yes."

"I've got aspirin in my desk. I'll get some."

"Kristal's asleep in there," Isabel reminded him. "I'll be fine." She looked down at her hands. "How's Marcia?"

"Gone." He went to the tree he'd brought in earlier and had forgotten about until now. "I thought the office should have a Christmas tree and that we should have a little party with the men tomorrow. What do you think?"

"Fine." She didn't really care about a party just then. She cared about... "Is everything all right again with you and...and her?"

"We parted friends, if that's what you're asking."

What *was* she asking, Isabel wondered, and didn't know. She did know, however, that his reply was completely unsatisfactory.

"You'll see her again, then?"

"No doubt." On his knees now, Eric rummaged in the large brown bag he'd carried in along with the tree, and pulled out several boxes of ornaments. "Come on, help me decorate this thing."

"Did she give you her present?" Isabel heard herself probe. She seemed unable to let the subject drop.

Something in the tightness of her voice made Eric raise his head. Settling back on his heels, he stared at her. She refused to meet his gaze. A light clicked on in his brain. Of course. A swell of happiness surged through him.

"You're jealous," he pronounced.

"What!" As if stung by a hornet, Isabel surged to her feet. Red heat suffused her face.

More sedately, Eric, too, got to his feet. "I said—"

"You couldn't be more wrong." *Jealous,* Isabel thought, appalled. Good Lord, he was right.

He walked slowly toward her. "It's all over your face." He reached across the desk to lay his hand along a flushed cheek.

She jerked back. "Don't."

"Why not?" Eric suddenly felt an overpowering need to break down her barriers and release the passionate woman she kept imprisoned behind them. And he knew just how to do it.

"Afraid?" he taunted softly.

Isabel predictably bristled. "Of you? That'll be the day."

He shook his head, taking a step closer. "Not of me, Isabel," he murmured. "Of yourself." He walked around the desk and stopped just inches from her.

Eric was so close Isabel felt enveloped by the heat radiating from his body. The urge to run was powerful, but an equally powerful force kept her rooted. She felt compelled to argue that she knew no fear, period. But one, that would be a lie, and two, her tongue seemed as paralyzed as her legs. His gaze bored into her with the intensity of a laser beam, but she refused to meet it.

"Marcia and I were finished even before she came here today," Eric said, his eyes on the shimmering crown of Isabel's bent head. "I followed her outside merely to bid her the kind of civilized goodbye she deserves. She's a very nice woman, Isabel. I like her very much."

Isabel's glorious hair seemed to beg for his touch; he'd wanted to bury his hands in it from the first time he'd seen it. He shaped his palm to the back of her head. "But I like you better."

Isabel gasped. She lifted her head and Eric's fingers slid down to the clip at the base of her skull. Unclasping it, he released the wavy tumble of her hair. He combed his fingers through its silken sun-streaked richness, then grasped a handful in his fist.

"I'm going to kiss you, Isabel," he murmured, urging her face toward his with gentle pressure against the back of her head. He drew her closer, bending toward her as he did, but slowly, to give her time to protest. To stiffen, to pull back.

She didn't.

Isabel, too, had realized in a flash of insight that the kiss they were about to share had been a long time coming. And that she wanted it. Desperately.

Just this once she'd let it happen, she told herself. Just this once she'd stop being cautious long enough to find out what Eric felt like, tasted like. Just this once. She had dreamed of it, imagined it, been afraid of it. But she wasn't afraid now.

She felt his breath on her lips and a shiver of reaction puckered her skin. She felt his hand massage her scalp and she couldn't stifle a moan of pleasure. She, too, lifted a hand, needing to caress as he caressed her. Their mouths were mere inches apart. She stroked his cheek, gloried in the masculine roughness of it. And then their lips touched.

It was like nothing either of them had ever experienced.

The initial contact jolted them with the force of an electrical shock. They jerked apart to stare into each other's darkened eyes, and then, with a groan, Eric wrapped both arms around Isabel's pliant form and hauled her against his taut body. His lips covered hers with an urgency and need no other woman had ever aroused in him.

He took the kiss deeper, and Isabel welcomed the touch of his tongue against hers. Sweetly, they tangled, his tongue and hers, and Isabel's bones turned to liquid. She allowed herself to melt into Eric's strength, just for a moment. She wanted to savor the feelings he aroused just a little longer. She wanted to commit them to memory so that she might relive them during lonelier times. Her senses swam, her thoughts became sluggish. She never wanted the kiss to end, but with a last shred of reason knew that it must. But not quite yet. In a moment...

The squeak of a door and a startled gasp, followed by a noisy clearing of the throat, accomplished what Isabel's weakened resolve had not been able to. Reason returned on a frigid draft of outside air.

Wrenching her lips from Eric's, she covered them with trembling fingers. She would have leapt back, but Eric's embrace wouldn't allow it. Shifting her mortified gaze from his slowly dawning grin to Frank LeFleur's startled expression, she longed for the floor to open up and swallow her.

What must Frank think went on in the company's front office? He knew about Arnie Mott, knew how Isabel felt about men, about being touched. What would he make of seeing her like this, wrapped around the boss's body like a sheet of plastic? How could she make clear to him that this wasn't what it seemed?

Just what is it then, Isabel?

Her inner voice asked the question, not Frank. Frank was looking at a spot above their heads now, and Isabel heard a chuckle begin to rumble from his chest. Her own gaze, too, flew ceilingward.

Mistletoe. Eric was holding a sprig of it up over their heads.

She met his sparkling eyes and knew a curious mixture of relief and disappointment. Mistletoe had prompted him to kiss her, nothing else. She searched his gaze, but found neither confirmation nor denial there.

"Merry Christmas" was all Eric said. Before Isabel could protest, and while Frank smilingly watched, he kissed her again, quickly, hard, then stepped back and released her. He rounded the desk and clapped his foreman on the shoulder.

"Executive privilege, my friend," he quipped with a wink. "Maybe you'll get your chance tomorrow night at the party."

Chapter Seven

He shouldn't have done it, of course. Eric knew that now. Hell, he'd known it even before he'd kissed her, but the accumulated need to taste and feel her had overpowered good sense. He told himself it was better this way. That knowing just how volatile things could be between himself and Isabel Mott was better than always wondering.

A load of bull if ever there was one.

Knowing was worse. Much worse. Knowing made him lie awake nights, wanting. Wanting her, wanting more. Wanting it all.

Knowing was keeping him at home, alone and sleepless, on, of all nights, New Year's Eve.

He paced, measured the length of his bedroom for the umpteenth time for the umpteenth day since their kiss. His chuckle was mirthless, derisive. *Since their kiss.* He, a man of science, a businessman, a mature adult, had been reduced to measuring time not as others did—A.D. or B.C.—but by S.K. Since Kiss. It was ridiculous.

Eric slammed a fist into the palm of his other hand. This had to stop. Isabel Mott was his secretary. He had to be crazy to contemplate an affair with her, and even crazier to contemplate anything more. Marriage? To Isabel Mott? He'd laugh if he weren't aching for her the way he was.

It was lust, that was all. And unrequited lust, at that.

Isabel had been not only cool, but downright aloof since that day, which ought to make it clear how she felt. On the job she was efficient and polite. Polite! He couldn't stand it. Since they'd met she'd hardly ever been polite to him. Now he missed the barbs, the flashes of temper, that husky, sometimes mocking laugh of hers.

At the Christmas party she'd stuck like glue to Frank and Joan LeFleur. The only thing she'd taken care to avoid more than Eric had been the sprig of mistletoe dangling from the ceiling. Had it reminded her of their kiss—as it had him? And was the memory so unpleasant she couldn't risk having the deed repeated?

No, dammit.

Eric scowled out into the darkness. He might not understand what made Isabel tick half the time, but he did know her response to him had been genuine. And far more passionate than he'd ever imagined it would be. He wanted it again, wanted more. Needed more. He needed to know if what they shared, what he'd felt, had been reality or merely a fluke. He doubted he'd ever get the chance to find out, though.

If only he hadn't returned the lovely silk scarf that had been his original Christmas gift to her. He'd bought it weeks earlier in one of Vancouver's most exclusive shops. But then, when Isabel had come to work for him and he'd been brought face-to-face with his conflicting emotions, he'd thought the gift too personal. And so, when it came time to exchange presents, he and Isabel discovered that they'd bought each other identical pen-and-pencil sets.

Even now, recalling that awkward moment and the stilted way they'd thanked each other, he cringed. Dammit, they should have been able to laugh about it. Would have laughed, if not for that kiss.

Eric lay down on the bed and folded his hands beneath his head. That kiss. His eyes drifted shut, not in sleep but in dreamy contemplation. She had tasted of honey, smelled like wildflowers, and her pliant heat had warmed him like summer sunshine. All too briefly an ardent flame of passion had ignited in her. He'd felt it in the press of her body against his, in the way her hands had convulsively clutched at his back and held him.

He'd felt her struggle to douse that flame even before Frank had made his untimely entrance.

She'd been hurt. Not then, not by him, but before. By someone else. Eric's eyes snapped open as unaccustomed rage tensed his muscles as if for combat. Why, he'd like to kill that son of a—

Wearily, he subsided back against the pillow. Though he'd give his life to protect or avenge the people he loved, at heart he was no fighter in the physical sense. But even if he were, there was no way in heaven or hell that Isabel Mott would let him or any man fight her battles.

Which was the crux of his dilemma, wasn't it? He was drawn to her as to no other woman before her. Worse, he knew it would take just the merest nudge to fall in love with her. But he also knew that in the unlikely event she'd agree to marry him, he'd be miserable ever after. Their values were miles apart, diametrically opposed. They weren't suited. It was as simple, and as complicated, as that.

He envisioned the perfect mate as someone domestic, someone compliant and agreeable. Isabel Mott was none of those things. Where he wanted someone to take care of, someone manageable, Isabel wanted to manage. Where he wanted ever after, Isabel wanted never again.

He knew all that. And still he couldn't sleep. Grimly, he got up and got dressed.

Isabel supposed it probably could've been worse. Kristal could have contracted chicken pox during Christmas while Delores was staying with them. According to the telephone conversation they'd just had, Delly had never had chicken pox.

Of course, neither had Isabel.

Her head hurt. Kristal had finally drifted into sleep after hours of fretting and Isabel longed to close her own eyes, as well. But she didn't dare. What if the baby woke up and needed her? No, no, best to stay awake. Shivering, she drew the heavy quilt up over her nose. She forced herself to concentrate on the old movie playing on television. Lovers were kissing.

Isabel thought of Eric and a wave of reaction caused a different kind of shiver. She hadn't been able to relax around him since that kiss beneath the mistletoe. It seemed as if with the crumbling of one set of walls, another set had been erected. The more she felt herself drawn to Eric, the higher she stacked her defenses.

She wondered which of the names on his telephone list was his date on this special night. With Marcia out of town, was he with Lois, who occupied the number-two slot? Or was Jocelyn the lucky one? Or Carla? Were they dancing in some posh club? Had they dined somewhere special first, or gone to the theater? Was he kissing her, long and deep, as the screen lovers were kissing?

As he'd kissed her?

Isabel snatched up the remote and flicked off the TV. Her eyes burned. She was itchy—and so hot. She tossed off the quilt. Her head hurt. So did her heart. Kristal cried out.

Isabel tottered off the sofa and toward the kitchen. With hands that shook she filled a bottle with a mixture of juice and water, splashing some on the floor and on herself in the process. Only one clean bottle left, she noted dismally. And no more juice at all. She hated herself for the miserable housekeeper she was.

She dragged herself toward the nursery, murmured to her baby as she held her close and let her drink. Kristal fell asleep again halfway through the bottle. It took all of Isabel's strength to put her back in the crib.

She felt like a rag doll, all limp, without starch. What muscles she seemed to have ached. She hugged the walls for support, bracing herself against waves of dizziness as she fought her way back to the living room.

"Eric," she whimpered, "help me..." And then the floor rushed up and hit her.

Eric had walked briskly and for quite a long time. It was a clear night, and stars could be seen in the few dark patches of sky not obscured by city lights. It was cold. Frost pinched the end of his nose, and his breath came out in puffs of steam. He strode along with no particular destination in mind. Just to move felt good; in any case better than tossing, wide awake and restless, alone in his bed.

As he went, he passed several clubs with New Year's Eve celebrations still in full swing. Snatches of music wafted out to him on clouds of hot and stale air through open doors. Bursts of laughter, the blare of noisemakers, all attested to the good time everyone was having. In years past he, too, had loved to be among the merrymakers till dawn's early light.

The new year was nearly an hour old when he crossed Granville Street Bridge, leaving the west end, downtown, and the revelers behind. Now he found himself below and just to the east of the bridge—in front of Isabel Mott's condominium.

Hands buried in the pockets of his sheepskin jacket, chin tucked into the collar he'd drawn up around his ears, Eric scowled up at her windows. They were ablaze with lights. It seemed Ms. Mott was throwing quite a party. He'd never have thought her the type.

His lip curled in self-derision. Since when was he the expert on Isabel's type? Come to that, he doubted she was one. Surely they'd thrown away the mold after creating the redoubtable Ms. Mott; certainly *he* had never encountered anyone even remotely like her.

It was awfully quiet for a party.

He took a few steps closer to the building. Silence. His scowl deepened and something like a premonition made the hair at the back of his neck stand up. Even with double-paned windows and all of them shut, couldn't sounds from a party usually be heard out on the street? Or at least, shouldn't he be seeing guests moving past the well-lit windows now and then?

Unless all of them had passed out in drunken stupors.

A grim smile negated the notion. Isabel Mott might be many things, but a drunk she wasn't. Nor would she have drunken friends, he'd bet on it.

Perhaps she couldn't sleep, either.

The thought perked him right up. Perhaps she'd like company. Could be she'd like to talk. He sure would.

Eric hesitated, though every fiber within him seemed to want to drag him inside. It was laughable, of course, but he felt suddenly as if Isabel needed him. As if she was in there waiting for him. Hoping he'd come...

He was at her door in three long strides. Gently he knocked. And then louder. Nothing. Or, wait—was someone calling out to him?

He pressed his ear to the door, straining to hear. His heart was suddenly beating so hard the sound of it drowned out everything else. He sucked in a harsh breath and held it, hoping to control his pulse as he pressed closer still. Nothing. Only silence. But he could swear he'd heard something.

"Isabel?" Eric rattled the door knob. "Can you hear me? Open the door."

He heard a moaning sound. Was it closer than before? Was it moving toward the door?

Eric froze. Ice formed in his veins and a terrible fear constricted his throat. She had called out to him. She needed him. And there was no way he could get to her. Or was there? Frantic, he dashed around the house, along the lower windows, checking them. All were closed, as was the door to the basement garage. He sprinted back up the steps, pounded on the door.

"Isabel? Can you hear me? Can you open this door?" *Where the hell would she hide a spare key?*

With hands that shook, he checked the obvious places. Under the doormat. Nothing. On the ledge above the door. Nothing. Behind the carriage light next to the door. Bingo!

Even as he congratulated himself and fumbled the key into the lock, he vowed to blister her ears for hiding a key where anyone could so easily find it. But first...

He stormed inside and was on his knees beside Isabel's crumpled form in seconds. "Isabel."

He cupped her face and gasped. She was burning up. But she was conscious. At his touch her eyelids fluttered, slowly lifted. Her eyes were overbright with fever, her lips dry as she tried to speak.

He hushed her. But she persisted. "K-kristal," she finally managed to croak.

The baby. Eric's head snapped up and he strained to hear, but all was silent. "She's sleeping," he assured Isabel. "Here, let me get you into bed, too."

"N-no," Isabel breathed, looking frantic and clutching at his arm. "Ch-check on her. P-please..."

"All right." Reluctant to leave her, yet afraid she might harm herself by becoming upset if he didn't comply, Eric rose. He'd never been at Isabel's, but the place wasn't very large and he had no trouble finding the nursery. He tiptoed up to the crib. Kristal's breathing was noisy and she felt hot to the touch, but she was blessedly asleep.

Fond as he was of the little girl, Eric instantly dismissed her from his mind and hurried back to the mother. Isabel lay where he'd left her, eyes closed again, her breathing shallow. She was sick, that much was clear, but with what?

Feeling helpless and inadequate, Eric felt her forehead, stroked her cheek. "Isabel," he whispered, "let me help you to bed and then I'll call a doctor."

He could see the effort it cost her to open her eyes and look at him. It wrenched his heart. She licked dry lips and mumbled something he couldn't understand.

"What?" He leaned closer, put his ear practically against her mouth.

"Ch-chicken pox," he thought she said. Lifting his head, he looked at her and repeated the words.

She nodded her head. "H-have you h-had...?"

"Have I had chicken pox?" The question seemed so silly. What did it have to do with—Damnation!

"Are you saying you think you have chicken pox?" he asked, shocked. It was a childhood disease and of course he'd had it. An itchy business, he seemed to recall. Nothing major in the way of illnesses. For children. But what did the virus do to adults? He'd read that measles could render an adult male sterile....

He saw her nod and thought, Good God, could this thing be equally harmful?

Without further talk or ceremony, he scooped Isabel up in his arms and took her to the only other room he'd seen besides the living room, nursery and, in passing, the kitchen. His hunch proved correct. It was Isabel's bedroom. The significance of being in it was lost on him under the circumstances, though he did, peripherally, notice that the bed was unmade and that every item of furniture in the room seemed to be covered with . . . stuff.

At any other, less critical time he'd have called her bedroom a disaster.

Just then, though, all Eric could think of calling was a doctor. He did so from Isabel's bedside, after he'd carefully laid her flannel-nightie-clad form on the bed and covered her with the quilt he'd found on the living-room floor.

"Mike."

Thank God, Mike Sloan had had night duty the week before and was now at home. Also asleep, but what did it matter? They were friends. Mike was a resident at Vancouver General Hospital, and he and Eric had been pen pals long before Eric had ever thought of leaving his country for Canada. Perhaps Mike had been a factor in making up Eric's mind; certainly his friendship had helped make Eric's assimilation into a new and younger culture easier. At this stage of their friendship, however, none of that mattered. Eric had been best man at Mike's wedding, and had helped build their West Vancouver house. Had been told he'd be godfather to the child Mike and Sunny were expecting.

They were friends.

"I have an emergency," Eric told him. "Can you come right over?"

There was no question but that Mike could. Eric gave him the address and directions and hung up, feeling much better. Mike was on the way. Mike was the best. Wasn't he a pediatrics resident? Who better to know about chicken pox?

Isabel had fallen asleep or passed out, Eric didn't know which. He forced himself not to panic, not to fuss with her, touch her, hold her as he longed to do. Logic dictated he force himself to remain calm until Mike arrived and gave him instructions as to how to be of productive help. Meanwhile...

Eric wandered out of Isabel's chaotic bedroom into Kristal's immaculately tidy one. Even in the half illumination from the hall light, Eric could discern neat stacks of diapers next to talcum, wipes and salve on the changing table. He saw carefully hung Disney prints and orderly shelves of stuffed toys and books. In an open closet her little outfits hung in a tidy row. Satisfied that Kristal was still breathing the deep breaths of sleep, he wandered back out...

...into Isabel's living room. If it could be called that. Scanning tabletops, chairs, sofa and shelves littered haphazardly with books, magazines, mugs, baby bottles and shoes, Eric would hardly call the place livable.

Shoes? He did another quick inspection and count. There were thirteen shoes scattered here and there.

Thus forewarned, he risked only a quick peek into the kitchen.

He blanched, could actually feel the blood drain from his face in horrified amazement at the sight that greeted him. Not an inch of counter space was clear of dishes. There was not, as far as Eric could see, a single dish free of abundant leftovers. Not only did the woman obviously not bother to eat more than a bird, she also didn't bother to save and store her leftovers. Or clean up after herself in any way at all.

Eric had never seen the like.

How could a woman like Isabel Mott, a woman whose snack truck had been the model of cleanliness and who had sold home-baked goodies to his men, have a kitchen like this? How could Isabel Mott, a woman who was death on misfiled memos and cluttered desks, tolerate such utter chaos in her private life?

Eric had no idea. None, that is, except to make sure things were set to rights. Here, at last, was something constructive he could do while he waited for Mike to show up. His movement brisk with purpose, he rolled up his sleeves.

And picked up the phone.

"Frau Schultz?"

Just as soon after coming to Canada as financial circumstances allowed, Eric had hired Mrs. Eva Schultz as his housekeeper. He'd been raised to love and respect order in a household but, being male, had neither expected nor been trained to bring such order about for himself. Women did these things so much better, his mother had told him the one time he'd dusted the parlor furniture and accidentally shattered her favorite vase. After all, it was women's work; it was their job. He'd never meddled in that job again. And, of course, it didn't occur to him to do so now, except to call in an expert.

Eva, a second-generation Irish immigrant, was a frustrated mother. Unable to have children with her seafaring husband, who was of German extraction, and alone for months at a time while he was at sea, she was delighted to have someone to pamper. And she adored the courtly way her Mr. Rudy always called her *Frau* Schultz.

On the phone with her now, Eric sat down on Isabel's living-room couch, found it lumpy and lifted his rear. Feeling around beneath himself, he extracted a wire whisk, a hammer and a staple gun. Brows raised in puzzlement as he studied his find, he spoke into the phone. "This is an emergency. Can you come right over?"

She could.

Relieved to have been able to call in the most qualified people to handle the situation, Eric was anxious now to be close to Isabel until the doctor arrived. He walked quietly up to her bed and his heart constricted at the sight of her lying there so small and helpless. He took the hand that was dangling limply over the side of the bed. It was hot and dry. How small it felt in his. How vulnerable.

Isabel didn't react to his touch. Her eyes were closed. Still holding her hand, his eyes riveted on her fever-flushed face, Eric sat down on the edge of the mattress. He touched her forehead—hot, so hot.

There must be something he could do for her. With something like desperation, Eric looked around. His eyes lit on the bathroom door, and he thought, *That's it, a washcloth.* Whenever he'd been ill as a child, his mother had laid a damp washcloth on his forehead and it had felt so good.

Gently releasing Isabel's hand, Eric rushed into the bathroom. Moments later he was back at her bedside and carefully arranging the cloth across her feverish brow.

Isabel flinched, then flung her head from side to side as if trying to shake off the cloth. It slipped and lay in a soggy heap on her pillow. Her eyes flew open. Wildly, she stared at Eric who was reaching across her to retrieve the wash-cloth.

"Don't touch me," she snarled. "Don't come near me or touch me ever again."

Eric felt as if he'd been slapped. He jerked back, and was on his feet and staring down into the mask of hatred her face had become. Good Lord, what did she think he'd meant to do?

"Isabel," he croaked. "I'd never do anything to hurt you."

"Ha!" Isabel sneered. She snapped upright, tore at the front of her flannel nightgown. The buttons popped, and she bared her chest.

Eric stood frozen, too horrified to do more than stare.

"Never hurt me." Isabel clawed the gown off her shoulders. "You drunken coward, look at these bruises. Why don't you pick on someone your own size?"

In the quick glance with which Eric scanned her bared torso, he saw no bruises. Whatever harm had been done her must have been done long enough ago for the physical marks to have faded. Her terror and fury sparked a rage in him the like of which he'd never felt before. Who had hurt her? Whom did she see, staring at him as at some vile snake?

"Isabel—"

"No." She pointed a shaking finger at the door. "You get away from me, d'you hear me? Get out, Arnie. Get out or I'll call the police. GET OUT!"

Arnie.

Rather than distress Isabel further, Eric left the room. His thoughts were racing. Who was this Arnie she hated so? This Arnie who had beaten her? This Arnie he'd like to get his hands on and slowly kill?

In the middle of the living room he stopped, raked trembling fingers through his hair and looked wildly around as if he might find some clue to the man's identity.

Pictures. Moving swiftly, Eric looked for pictures, family photos. There weren't any. What he did bump into on the floor in one corner, however, were some half dozen canvases leaning haphazardly against the wall. Also a folded paint-splattered easel, brushes and other painting paraphernalia. Frowning, Eric picked up the closest canvas and gasped in surprise at the beauty of it.

It was a child's face. It was Kristal, serenely sleeping. Downy blond curls kissed her dimpled baby cheeks, her delicate pink bow of a mouth was sweetly parted.... Eric's eyes flew to the signature. There wasn't one.

Someone was knocking on the door.

Mike. Finally. Dropping the painting where he'd found it, Eric rushed to the door.

"What took you so long?" he accused, dragging his friend inside, which was no easy task since Mike Sloan was fully six foot five and used to be a linebacker in college.

Reddish brows shot up into an even redder thatch of hair as Mike glanced pointedly at his watch. "Fifteen minutes from dead sleep to here is long?"

"It is when the patient is delirious."

"Oh?" Mike allowed himself to be ushered along. "What makes you think she is?"

"She yelled at me to get out, for one."

"Means she has good taste," Mike drawled, and earned himself a scathing glare. "What is she to you?" he asked.

"My, um . . . my secretary."

"Oh?" Mike stopped to eye his friend curiously and resisted Eric's attempts to move him farther. "This promises to be interesting, old buddy."

"This also promises to be the end of our friendship if you don't get yourself in to see her this instant," growled Eric. He nodded toward Isabel's door. "In there. I'll wait out here."

"Good idea." Unperturbed by his friend's barely leashed temper, Mike ambled into Isabel's room.

"Get out!" she greeted him, and even though Eric had already known earlier that her invective had been nothing against him personally, he felt a measure of relief at hearing it now directed at Mike, whom she didn't know at all.

It was 5 a.m. Isabel had been medicated and made comfortable. She was now asleep. Frau Schultz had done a cursory tidying of the living room and now was noisily attacking the kitchen.

Mike had left. He'd confirmed Isabel's self-diagnosis of chicken pox, calmly adding that it seemed to have progressed into a case of encephalitis, which explained the high fever and attendant delirium.

"Bed rest, lots of fluids and good nutrition is about all we can do for her," Mike had told Eric, adding that it might well be several weeks before Isabel was well again. He had pronounced Kristal over the worst of it.

He had also pressed Eric into promising they'd get together at their earliest convenience, at which time he intended to find out the precise nature of Eric's relationship with Isabel Mott.

"Secretary, my scalpel," he'd declared.

Knowing the futility of trying to convince his friend that there was nothing to know, Eric had ushered Mike out as eagerly as he'd earlier ushered him in. Then he'd given

Kristal a soda bath, which had left him, as well as the bathroom floor, drenched. After gently toweling her dry, leaving the bathroom for Frau Schultz to clean, he had dabbed calamine lotion on her pox blisters, then diapered and dressed her.

Now he had her in a high chair and was trying to feed her pureed pears and rice cereal. Kristal was having a grand old time.

Eric was sweating bullets and already wearing the better part of Kristal's meal.

"Just one more bite for Uncle Eric," he coaxed for the umpteenth time, and congratulated himself as the baby obediently opened her mouth. She allowed him to put the spoon inside, then closed her mouth and clamped down on the spoon with her two front teeth.

Eric gently wiggled it. "Let go, sweetheart, there's my girl."

Behind him, Eva Schultz chuckled.

"What's so funny?" Eric grumbled without turning. The spoon was still in Kristal's mouth and she was grinning at him impishly as if she knew she had him just where she wanted him.

"You are, Mr. Rudy," Eva said, drying dishes and putting them away. "The two of you. I'd never have thought you so paternal."

"I've always liked children." In spite of his fatigue—after all it was five o'clock in the morning—Eric couldn't help but grin back at Kristal as he gently tugged on the spoon yet again. "Let go, baby."

She did. And immediately pursed her lips to noisily spray the spoonful of pears out at Eric.

With spoon in hand and pears on his face, he wearily turned to his housekeeper. "Frau Schultz . . ."

She turned, saw his face, and giggled.

"Could I impose upon you to clean her up and put her to bed while I do the same for myself?"

"Certainly, Mr. Rudy."

"Thank you."

Bone-tired, Eric dragged himself into the bathroom for a quick wash. Then he stumbled into the living room and onto the couch. He was asleep before his head even hit the pillow with the fourteenth shoe under it.

Eight days later it was Saturday and the first day Isabel was to be allowed out of bed. She looked forward to it the way a child looked forward to Christmas. Lying in bed, weak as a kitten, while R. E. Schwenker made like a dictator and his, admittedly wonderful, Frau Schultz like a prison-warden-cum-nursemaid was not her idea of a good time. Enough already.

"I'll wear the velour jumpsuit," she told Eva, who'd just helped with Isabel's first real shower in more than a week.

"A robe would be better, love," Eva countermanded her, already taking Isabel's arm and stuffing it into a sleeve. "Easier to get in and out of, you know."

"But…" Isabel began to protest, then wearily let it drop. What was the use of arguing, she thought on a wave of self-pity. They'd do with her what they wished, anyway. And she was in no shape yet to stop them.

"I've made you some nice chicken soup," Eva was saying as she started to tie Isabel's belt.

"Yuck," said Isabel, crankily pushing the older woman's hands out of the way. "And I can tie my own belt, thank you."

Eva tut-tutted. "Mr. Rudy said not to let you overdo, love."

"Mr. Rudy can take a flying leap." Isabel fumbled with the belt, her hands beginning to shake from weakness and agitation. "Oh, damn . . ."

"There, love, I'll do it," Eva said gently.

"I hate this," Isabel exclaimed with a quaver in her voice, and was further horrified by the realization that any second now she'd burst into tears. What was the matter with her?

"Soon you'll be better," Eva soothed, bending to put warm slippers on Isabel's feet. She straightened, took Isabel's hand. "There now, are we ready?"

Isabel nodded. What she really felt ready for by then was another nap, but no way was she going to admit that to anyone. They'd have her back in bed so fast it'd make her head spin even more than it already did, and she couldn't stand the thought of it. She had to get out of this room for a while.

Gratefully she accepted Eva's hand as she slowly shuffled on rubbery legs out into the hall.

"Where's Kristal?"

"In the living room with Mr. Rudy."

What would I have done without him? Isabel thought. Eric had been there every day, leaving Eva with her for the hours he was forced to go to the office. He'd slept every night on the living-room sofa.

I'm deeply in his debt. The realization made Isabel acutely uncomfortable. She didn't like to be indebted to anyone. Least of all to R. E. Schwenker. Owing him favors made trying to understand and coming to grips with what she felt for him even more complicated.

At the arched opening into the living room Isabel stopped with a gasp. "Omigosh!" she exclaimed, eyes wide.

Eric, reclining in the stuffed chair with Kristal on his lap, dropped *Engineering Weekly,* the magazine from which he'd been reading to the little girl, to the floor.

"Isabel!" His heart swelled at the sight of her. Scooping Kristal up like a football, he scrambled to his feet. "Here, let me help you."

"What on *earth* have you done to this room?"

"Beg your pardon?" Caught completely off guard, Eric stared into Isabel's distraught face, then scanned the room. It looked perfect.

Eva, too, turned rounded eyes on her charge. "I've only tidied and cleaned it, love."

"It's awful," Isabel wailed. And then her worst fears were realized: she who never cried, burst into tears.

Eric reacted as if he'd been electrocuted. Everything in him quivered with empathy and concern. He was at her side in two long strides, thrusting Kristal into Eva's arms.

"Take her somewhere, Frau Schultz." He reached for Isabel, scooped her up in his arms. She made no protest, only buried her face against his neck.

Eric carried her shivering form back to the bedroom, crooning meaningless words that were meant to soothe and comfort. Isabel couldn't stop the silent tears from flowing; they came relentlessly as if from a faucet.

Eric had looked so at home, so *right,* sitting in that easy chair reading to her daughter.

It was *that* which had upset her. Taking exception to the practically sterile condition of the room had merely been the guise in which to cloak her dismay.

She wanted to cling to Eric, tell him to keep holding her, never to leave her. She struggled feebly in his arms, and croaked, "Please put me down."

Gently he lowered her to her feet, but kept one arm around her for support while his free hand swiftly untied the knot of her belt.

Isabel pushed him away. "I can do it," she said. And shakily tried. Eric's large warm hand covered both of hers, stilling and firmly moving them aside.

Isabel made no further protest as he slipped the robe off her. Her limbs and knees were jelly, and without Eric there to hold her she would have collapsed.

Eric tossed the robe aside, intent on doing what was needed for Isabel, and even more intent on not reacting to the feel of her skimpily clad body against his own.

You're an animal, he fiercely chided himself. To even remotely feel lust for a woman in Isabel's pitiful condition was an outrage.

It did no good, this harangue. The wanting, the need, only increased as he once again lifted her in his arms and placed her on the bed like a priceless treasure. He allowed himself one quick look, one brief instant to savor the sight of those tantalizing peaks and valleys, which were all the more enticing because they were barely veiled by the satiny fabric of her gown.

Eric gripped the quilt and jerked it right up to Isabel's chin. He glanced at her face—had she seen him staring? Something flickered in her eyes, now dry, and he knew that she had.

"Isabel . . ."

"Please go away," she whispered and closed her eyes.

Eric stared at her a moment longer, wanting to protest, wanting to explain. But what?

He bit his lip, slowly straightened. "I'll see you tomorrow."

Yes, Isabel thought dreamily, almost asleep. Tomorrow. "No!" She opened her eyes. She had to stop being dependent on him. It felt too right when she knew it was all wrong.

Again she cried no. But it came out as only a whisper and, anyway, Eric had already left the room.

Chapter Eight

Getting up the next day was much easier. Some starch was gradually coming back into Isabel's limbs.

"My chicken soup will do wonders for you," Eva said. "Mr. Rudy, make sure she drinks all of it."

"I will." He winked at Isabel, ensconced on the couch, then smiled at his housekeeper. "Don't worry about a thing. You and Kristal have a good time."

The day was sunny; Eva and the child were headed out for a walk. Eric carried the stroller outside, made sure Kristal was safely strapped into it, then hurried back to Isabel.

"Alone at last," he quipped, rubbing his hands as he entered the living room.

Isabel smiled weakly. "Should I be worried?"

Their eyes met. Unspoken messages made the air between them hum.

Isabel's heart fluttered. Her fingers tightened around the mug of chicken soup she was holding. She ducked her head, breaking the prolonged eye contact, and took a sip.

Eric cleared his throat, chafed his hands again. "It's nippy out there."

"Is it?" Isabel was intent on her soup. "The sun feels good in here, though."

"Sure does." He took a seat across from the couch.

They were silent. Both were aware that this was the very first time they'd ever been completely alone. At the office the men were always nearby. Here, in this apartment, there was only the two of them. In the kitchen the refrigerator motor kicked in with a hum. A clock ticked. Outside a dog's whine became an angry bark. Somebody laughed.

"Perhaps some music." Eric leaped to his feet, knelt in front of the shelf on which sat some stereo components. "What do you like?"

"Anything."

He tuned in an "oldies" station. "How's that?"

"Fine."

Eric straightened, turned. "How about some tea?"

"I've got this soup, thanks."

"Right." Eric playfully cocked a forefinger at her. "Better drink it, or else," he joked.

He stood irresolute, looking down at her, wondering how the hell to get past this awkwardness between them. "Isabel, what are we doing?"

She didn't pretend not to understand. "Being self-conscious, I think."

"But that's ridiculous! I ask you, after all we've been through together by now, what's left to be self-conscious about?"

"I don't know." Isabel set down the mug, taking care to keep her eyes on it. She knew very well what she was self-conscious about—being alone with Eric and the fact that she longed with every fiber of her being to take advantage of that.

Eric strode to the window and stared out into the street for long moments. A fierce debate was raging inside him. Here was his chance, part of him shouted. That was the part consumed by lust and wanting. Don't be a jerk, a saner part sneered. She's still your secretary. Remember you promised to leave well enough alone?

He turned to look at her. He drank in the flawless profile softened by the golden mane, streaked with sunbeams that caressed a flushed cheek. His gaze traced the length of her slender body, clad in a jumpsuit that lovingly clung to her every curve. And he knew that leaving it, leaving *her*, well enough alone was rapidly ceasing to be an option.

Maybe it was time, he thought, to bring the things that hovered between them out into the open.

"Isabel, look at me."

The husky timbre of Eric's voice touched Isabel like a caress. She lifted her eyes to his with the utmost reluctance, afraid of what she'd see there. And, at the same time, breathlessly expectant.

"You're so beautiful," he said when she faced him at last. "More beautiful than any other woman I know."

Isabel thought of the glamorous Marcia and doubted his words but soaked them up greedily just the same.

"I know this is probably not the time to say this," he added in a gruff voice, "but I have to say it, anyway."

Her eyes widened. He saw trepidation there, but sparks of desire, as well. His voice a husky whisper, he said, "I want you, Isabel."

Isabel's eyes closed. *Oh, Lord, I want you, too.* She swallowed helplessly. "Oh?"

Eric longed to rush to her, to cup the face that looked so apprehensive and kiss and caress it until it relaxed. But he stayed where he was. "How do you feel about that?"

Excited, Isabel thought, her heart in her throat. "Regretful," she said softly. She had to force the words out, knowing they would hurt him, but knowing, too, that she didn't dare let things go any further.

Eric's lips compressed. With a curt nod, he averted his eyes. "I see."

"No, you don't. Eric, it's not because of you. It's me. I just can't get involved."

Eric looked up to see the shadows of pain that darkened her eyes as she quietly added, "With anyone. Ever again."

They looked at each other in silence, but somehow the earlier tension between them had been diffused.

"Who's Arnie?" Eric quietly asked at length.

Shocked to hear him mention the name, Isabel's eyes widened. "How...?"

"You were delirious that first night." Eric frowned, finding it difficult even now to come to grips with that ugly scene and what he'd learned. "He beat you, didn't he?"

"Yes." Barely a whisper.

"My God!" Eric's hands balled into fists. "Isabel, who is he?"

Isabel wrenched her gaze from his. She looked down at her hands. They, too, were clenched into fists. "He was my husband."

Was. Eric swiftly crossed the room and knelt at her side. "Tell me."

"No." Isabel shook her head. "I don't want to talk about it. He's dead. Gone."

"But he isn't, don't you see?" Eric gripped her hand. "He's still with you. He's still in your life, ruining it. Tell me, Isabel, and let it go."

"All right." Isabel tugged her hand out of his. She was too weak to argue, and besides, maybe if Eric knew, he'd understand that there could never be more than friendship between them.

"Arnie was in an aerobics class I taught. Trying to get his body back into shape after a long illness, he said. An illness that had cost him his job. Everything."

She laughed in bitter recollection. "I didn't know until it was way too late that this illness of his was alcoholism. Or that he didn't want to be helped.

"When we met he was charming, warm, and because he was too sick to work yet—his story—he was always there for me. He moved in with me, pampered me, did the housework. You've seen what a terrible housekeeper I am...." She shrugged. "I thought he'd been sent straight from heaven."

Her tone became bitter again and she looked down at her hands. "Hell, more likely."

Tears threatened and she angrily forced them back. She'd vowed not to shed even one more tear over Arnie Mott and she wouldn't. She bit her lip, hard.

Eric's heart went out to her. "Isabel, if you don't—"

"No." She angrily shook her head. "I'm okay. I want you to hear it all now."

"All right, then."

She took a deep breath. "When he suggested we get married, it seemed like the perfect solution for both of us. I was healthy, had my own business, so I could be the breadwinner. In return, while he recuperated, he'd be the househusband. It could have been really good...."

Eric snorted. "No, it couldn't."

"It could," Isabel insisted. "It was. As long as he stayed sober."

"But he didn't." It was a statement, not a question.

"No."

"And when he drank he beat you?"

"Yes." The word was the merest whisper.

"Dammit, Isabel." Eric jumped to his feet, too filled with violent emotions to sit still any longer. "Why didn't you get out?"

"I did. I'd already filed for divorce when he was killed in an accident." She paused, again bit her lip to keep it from trembling. "I'd gotten to feeling so helpless, so afraid of his drunken rages that it took a while for me to work up the courage to seek a divorce, to stage the final scene. Get out, I was going to tell him. Get out and never come back."

Averting her face, she sucked in a ragged breath. "If only I'd had a chance to tell him that."

"You did tell him." Eric bent to her, gently gripped her chin and forced her to look at him. "You told him that the other night."

She searched his eyes. "I did?"

He nodded. "Yes." Their gazes clung. Hers softened and seemed to reflect the longings he felt.

"Isabel." Slowly he moved his head toward hers and whispered, "I'd never hurt you."

Her small laugh sounded all the more bitter for its softness. "Oh, Eric, don't you see? That's what he said, too."

If Isabel had slashed him with a knife, Eric couldn't have been more deeply wounded. He jerked away from her. How could she lump him, who'd never done her anything but kindness, in with the kind of men who abused women?

Yet he knew it wasn't her fault. Good God, her rejection wasn't even anything personal. She wasn't ready to trust any man and, hey, why should she trust him? Were his intentions honorable? Was he planning to marry her?

He didn't have to hear that cynical inner voice jeer, *Hell, no,* to know he was only a little bit less of a heel than Mott had been.

Suddenly he felt twice his age and bone-weary. These past nine days had been rough on him in terms of worry, the stress of wanting to be there for Isabel while needing to be at his place of business, too, and nights spent largely sleepless on Isabel's living-room couch. Had he put up with it all purely out of friendship? Or had he hoped to cash in on a budding "something more"?

It hurt to be honest with himself, but the truth of it was that in the course of taking care of her, he'd forgotten his resolution to keep their relationship on a business level. Because he was attracted to Isabel and because it had flattered him to think she was likewise attracted to him, he'd chosen to overlook that she was not the kind of woman he'd envisioned for a wife. But she wasn't a woman with whom he could merely have an affair, either. Right now he wasn't even sure she still could be a friend.

Stiffly, he got to his feet. "I think I'll make a cup of tea."

"Eric..."

"It's all right, Isabel. Let's leave it, shall we?" He walked out to the kitchen.

Watching his weary departure from the room, knowing she'd hurt him, Isabel wanted to cry. But tears seemed too easy, almost too trivial an expression of the deep kind of pain and regret she was feeling.

She lay back and closed her eyes, withdrawing into herself, shutting out the world, as she had always done when things became unmanageable. The trick had always worked for her when her father and mother were in the throes of one of their violent confrontations. Likewise with Arnie.

But it didn't work now. She could hear Eric in the kitchen slamming cupboard doors, and she could feel her own heart breaking. She could hear the ring of the telephone, and Eric's usually mellow baritone curtly answering it.

She opened her eyes. They connected with his as he walked in with the portable phone.

"It's your mother." He severed eye contact even before he turned and stalked back out to the kitchen. Isabel's thank-you went unheard, or at least, unacknowledged.

She swallowed, and slowly lifted the phone to her ear. "Mom?"

She paid scant attention to Delores's expressions of concern. As soon as her mother stopped talking, she blurted, "I need you, Mom." Her voice broke. "Can you come, please?"

Delly had been there in a matter of hours, and their week together since then had meant a lot to Isabel.

Eric had left the moment Eva Schultz and Kristal had returned from their outing. Eva had fed and bathed the little girl, and put her to bed. Then, at Isabel's adamant assurance that she'd be fine until her mother arrived, Frau Schultz, too, had departed.

Alone at last.

One moment that had resulted in a heartfelt exhalation, the next a painful reminder of Eric. That's what he'd said, jokingly, just before words like "want" and "can't" and "Arnie Mott" had gotten into the conversation. Nothing had been good since.

She longed for Eric, yet it was she who had rebuffed his attempt to move their relationship onto a more intimate plane. God help her, in the unlikely event he'd give it one more try, she would do it again.

It was all Arnie Mott's fault. Why had he died and cheated her out of at least having the satisfaction of tossing him out? Of knowing she did have it in her to stand up to him? This way, how could she ever be sure her courage wouldn't have failed her at the last moment? And not being sure, how could she respect herself?

Delores had been effusive in her delight to finally be needed by her only child. And during the past week of caring for Isabel, she'd been unflaggingly wonderful in the face of her patient's yo-yoing moods.

Isabel despised the inactivity and passivity her convalescence necessitated and was often quite vocal with her complaints. Other times, thinking of Eric, she was quietly depressed. He had called once to say he was keeping the job open for her should she want it, but that he'd understand if she didn't. She did want it. Needed it still, at least until she'd had a chance to figure out what to do about Kristal's care. But she spent hours agonizing over how she should act with him when she did return to the office, hours regretting, wishing and playing fruitless games of "what-if?" that only deepened her depression.

She had started knitting again. A man's sweater.

Delores had been as tolerant as a saint. She'd asked no questions, offered no advice. She'd done what needed doing and had minded her own business.

During those times—as now—when Isabel was totally at odds with herself and the world, her mother's very niceness was making her crazy.

"Mother." She yanked more yarn free of the skein.

Delores lowered the book she'd been reading. "Yes, dear?"

"Why are you being so good to me?"

Her mother sat up straighter, a guarded look on her face. "Pardon?"

"As far back as I can remember, I've been a perfect crab to you, not to use the 'B' word." Isabel furiously knitted, needles clicking. "Why are you still so good to me?"

"Darling, we've been through all that. You're my daughter." Delores shrugged, a gesture of helpless non-understanding. "I love you."

"Why?" Isabel demanded. She tossed down her knitting. "What is it about me that you love?"

"Lots of things..."

"Like what? That I look like my father?" Isabel swung her legs off the couch and started to pace. She stopped in front of her mother. "You ought to hate me for that."

"Well, I don't." Delores got to her feet, too. Her book dropped, unheeded, to the floor. She gripped Isabel's shoulders. "I don't."

Isabel searched her mother's eyes. "Do you hate...him?"

"No." Delores shook her head. "Not for a long time now."

"Oh, Mom..." Feeling remorse for all the bad thoughts she'd had, Isabel took her mother's hand and kissed the misshapen knuckles. "I used to blame you for making him angry...."

"Shh."

"No, let me say it. I used to think you had driven him away, made him leave me, and that you deserved it when he... And then when Arnie—"

"Don't, Isabel." Delores gave Isabel's shoulders a hard shake. "Don't say any more."

"But I—"

"No more, you hear me?" Delores's tone was adamant. "It's done. I wasn't to blame and neither were you. You know that." Her voice softened. "Isabel, listen to me." Her hands, trembling now, framed Isabel's averted face and pulled it around.

"There comes a time when the things that went before must cease to matter," she said with gentleness. "We should learn our lessons from the past, then let it go. I wish you could do that, child."

Looking into her mother's eyes and seeing the pleading there, Isabel wished she could, too. "I can't, Mom," she said sadly. "Not yet." She removed Delly's hands from her face. "Maybe not ever."

Without another word she walked out of the room and out of the apartment.

She stopped in front of the building, the chill wind reminding her that she had come out without a coat. She hugged her arms around herself and crossed the quiet street. She wouldn't stay out long, just long enough to clear her head.

Across from her condominium a path meandered down a grassy slope to the picturesque floating homes moored at False Creek. She followed it slowly, inhaling wintry city air that smelled of saltwater and fish, car exhaust and food cooking. She savored the varied scents, even if they were brought to her on a damp chill breeze. This was the first time she'd been outdoors in so long. She felt like a prisoner who'd just escaped a lengthy incarceration.

There was a bench ahead, and she walked up to it and dropped onto it. Straight across from her was her home. Turning the other way, she faced the imposing structure that was B.C. Place and the jagged skyline of the city with its backdrop of snowcapped mountains.

Granville Street Bridge loomed to the left of her. Beneath it, Granville Island Market with its many vendors, stores and restaurants was, no doubt, enjoying its usual bustling activity.

Across, and well to the west of the bridge, lived Eric Schwenker.

Isabel shivered. She chafed her arms, uttering a soundless little laugh. Even their homes, she was thinking—hers and Eric's—were miles and miles apart. Just as they themselves seemed to be on every issue that mattered.

Yet he'd been there for her—been here, at her home—the night she'd gotten ill! How? Why? Good grief, she'd never even thought to ask him.

Isabel leaped to her feet and hurried back to her apartment. She met her mother, coat in hand, at the door.

"Excuse me, Mom."

She rushed to the phone, punched out Eric's number, impatiently waited for him to answer.

"Schwenker." He sounded preoccupied.

"Just what were you doing at my house on New Year's Eve?" she burst out.

"What? Isabel...?"

"Yes." She waited and tried to get her heartbeat to slow down.

After a moment's hesitation he said, "I couldn't sleep, so I took a walk."

"All the way over here?"

"As it turned out, yes."

Isabel clutched the phone, staring straight ahead at the wall. She licked dry lips. "Meaning you didn't intend to come here when you started out?" she finally whispered.

"I don't know." His sigh was explosive. "Are you all right?"

"I'm fine." She wasn't at all sure that was true. "It just occurred to me that I hadn't even asked you...I mean...thanks, Eric."

"You're welcome."

Isabel only nodded. Very gently, very carefully, she placed the receiver back in its cradle. She stood for long moments, head bent. What did it all mean? What was she to think? It was so uncanny, the way he'd been here, almost as if—

No. She instantly dismissed the ridiculous notion that presented itself. That sort of stuff was for dreamers. She, however, was nothing if not a realist. It had been coincidence, that's all.

But when she turned and found herself face-to-face with Delores, she put her arms around her mother's neck and let her head fall forward.

"Oh, Mom," she whispered, "tell me what to think. What to do."

"I can't, child." Delly held her close. "But I hope that, in time, you'll figure it out for yourself."

Isabel pulled into her spot in front of Schwenker Engineering and slipped the gear into park. She didn't turn off the engine and made no move to get out of the car. She stared at the concrete wall in front of her and wondered how on earth she was going to walk into that office. So far her mother's hope had not been fulfilled—Isabel hadn't figured out a thing.

All she knew was that she was more deeply in Eric Schwenker's debt than ever, and that made what had transpired that afternoon in her apartment an even more painful episode. Eric deserved better than to be hurt by her; she owed him so much.

Isabel resolutely inhaled a lungful of air and vowed that she'd repay him by being the best darn secretary she knew how to be. It wouldn't be enough, couldn't ever be enough, but it was all she had it in her to give.

"You gonna sit there all day?" Frank LeFleur was pulling open her door.

"Frank!" Isabel impulsively gave him a hug. It didn't occur to her to marvel at how far she had come. Only a few short months ago she wouldn't have been able to bring herself to touch a man, much less give him a hug.

Frank awkwardly patted her back and, his voice gruff, said, "'Bout time you showed your face again, young lady." He backed away to squint at her. "You okay?"

"Yep." Isabel killed the engine. "Thanks for the flowers and candy. And the teddy bear for Kristal."

Picking up her purse and the box containing the sweater she had knitted for Eric, she slid out of the car.

"You're welcome." Frank stood aside. "So where is the little mite? I bet she's grown, eh?"

"And how. You'll see for yourself tomorrow. Today's my mother's last day with us, so she wanted to keep Kristal home."

Together they rounded Isabel's car and walked to the building.

Eric, watching from his office window, envied them their easy camaraderie. He'd been dreading Isabel's return almost as much as he'd been longing for it. Countless were the times he'd called himself an idiot for still dreaming about her, but dream of her he did. Yet he'd come to accept that dreams were dreams and reality something else entirely. He and Isabel had a working relationship. Period. From now on he'd do his damnedest to keep that in mind.

Craning his neck, he saw that Frank and Isabel were at the front door. Isabel waved as Frank went on toward the shop entrance, and then she was gone from view. In just a second she'd be in her office, and then she'd probably proceed into his.

Eric straightened his already straight tie, buttoned the single button of his suit jacket. He'd worn a suit today because it looked more formal, which best reflected the way he intended to act toward Isabel from now on. Friendly, sure, but businesslike.

He heard her door open and close. He hoped she wouldn't misconstrue the small bouquet of flowers he'd put on her desk. He wished now he hadn't done it.

Footsteps.

Eric was behind his desk in two strides. He unbuttoned his jacket, deciding there was such a thing as being too formal.

A quiet knock on the door.

Eric's heartbeat escalated. God, the room was stifling. Should he sit? Stay standing?

"Come in." He sat. Snatched up the nearest piece of paper.

Hearing Eric calmly bid her enter, Isabel squared her shoulders, took one more deep breath and stuck a smile on her face. She could be every bit as cool and collected as R. E. Schwenker.

Head high, she walked into his office. "Good morning."

Eric was engrossed in some report. Brows furrowed in concentration, without speaking or looking up, he held up a finger to bid Isabel wait while he read on.

Miffed, but not about to show it, Isabel stepped closer, her package in hand. She'd just give him this—*if* he could spare her a moment—and then she'd be about her duties.

As he read, she studied him. He looked very distinguished in the charcoal gray suit. Or, she amended with a twinge of almost maternal indulgence, he would if his hair didn't look as if he'd been raking all ten of his fingers through it against the grain.

He was still reading. Isabel leaned closer. What was so important he couldn't take a minute to be civil? She couldn't make out the writing and leaned closer still. It said . . .

Her eyes widened. Smothering laughter, she reached out, murmuring, "Allow me." She took the paper out of his hand, turned it one hundred and eighty degrees and handed it back. "I think you'll find it easier to read this way."

Eric's face flushed scarlet. With an oath, he tossed the paper down and slumped back in his seat. He rubbed a hand over his face, then squinted up at her with a wry chuckle. "See what you've reduced me to?"

"Me?" Isabel bit her lip, not sure how to react to the peculiar expression on his face. "I'm sorry, but—"

"Hell, so am I." He shook his head, grimacing. "Good Lord. The games people play . . ."

He stood, yanked off his coat and tie, then rounded the desk. Gripping Isabel's shoulders, he planted a kiss on her forehead. "There," he said. "I wanted to kiss you, and I'll damn well do it. Welcome back, Ms. Mott."

Isabel had been too nonplussed by the unexpected turn of events to do more than stand there stiffly. He'd done it again, she thought, dazed. Instead of being embarrassed, and furious because of it, he'd laughed at having his own case of nerves exposed. Most men would surely have considered the situation a loss of face and, at the very least, would have resented her for having brought it about.

Eric had been as anxious about this morning as she had. Isabel hugged the realization to herself. Overwhelmed by a wealth of feelings for this man, she pulled his face down to hers and kissed him hard on the mouth.

"There," she said, grinning, and stepped away. "It's good to be back."

They exchanged smiles, but took care not to let their gazes linger.

"Well." Eric briskly turned to his desk and picked up a plastic container. "Frau Schultz sent chicken soup."

Isabel accepted it with a groan. "I hate this stuff."

"That's what she said you'd say. I was told to tell you to drink it, anyway."

"But I'm better now," Isabel protested.

Eric shrugged. "Preventive medicine, she says."

"Grr."

"I'll tell her you said that."

They laughed, now feeling awkward with each other, after all.

"Oh." Isabel set down the soup and picked up the box she'd earlier laid on the drafting table next to Eric's desk. "This is for you. A small token of—" she shrugged, convinced once again that the gift was inappropriate "—you know. Thanks."

"You don't owe me any thanks, Isabel," Eric said quietly, his eyes on the box. "Nor anything else. I . . ."

I will always be there for you, he'd been about to say, but recalled his resolution just in time. A working relationship. Damn, it was hard to remember that when they were face-to-face, and when she looked so damn desirable in that softly flowing, green wool dress.

He looked up with a forced laugh. "Let's just say you were my good deed for the year and forget it, shall we?" He hefted the box. "Thank you."

Suddenly it was all too much. Isabel's presence, his feelings, this present from her he didn't want. He needed her to be gone from his office now, away from him before his carefully leashed emotions broke free.

He checked his watch. "Goodness, look at the time. Do you mind if I open this later, Isabel? I'm afraid I have a call to make that can't wait..."

At his abrupt change of tone and attitude, Isabel withdrew. "Of course," she said, masking her hurt. "I'm sure I've got work to do, too."

Feeling boorish and rotten, Eric watched her leave the room. As soon as the door clicked shut, he opened the package, then stared at the handsome hand-knit sweater. Slowly he lifted it, shook it out, admired it. Then he buried his face in it and thought with despair, *Dear God, where do we go from here?*

Kristal's boisterous presence in the office went a long way toward diffusing the charged atmosphere of the previous day. The little girl was frankly delighted to see Eric. Crowing her joy, she held her pudgy arms out to him. And when he'd taken her from Isabel, Kristal had given him one of her wet, open-mouthed baby kisses.

Eric had been deeply touched by this artless display of affection and had quite contentedly played with the little girl until she'd gotten tired.

Things went fine, sort of, for several weeks. If there was an atmosphere of constraint between Eric and Isabel, they both pretended not to notice. Likewise, neither let on that they were constantly and excruciatingly aware of each other physically, and that their nerves were becoming as tightly strung as high-tension wires.

And then, one early March morning, Kristal woke up with a temperature, a runny nose and a thoroughly miserable disposition. Isabel might have chosen to stay home with her child that day, if the payroll hadn't needed doing and if Eric hadn't had a string of interviews with prospective engineers lined up.

Kristal was a crab during the ride to work, and things rapidly deteriorated from there. Due to the interviews, the playpen in which she took her naps had been placed in Isabel's office for the day. At nap time Kristal was standing in it, shaking the sides and howling, as she had been for most of the morning. Sleep was apparently the last thing on her agenda. All of Isabel's efforts to calm her were in vain.

With her own nerves rapidly fraying, Isabel thought it best to ignore the child for a while. She was almost done with the payroll. Afterward, she'd take Kristal home.

The door to Eric's office was jerked open. Eric, his face wreathed in thunderclouds, came marching out and up to Isabel's desk. "For God's sake, can't you keep your child quiet? We can't hear ourselves think in there."

Isabel was instantly on the defensive. "I can't think much in here, either," she shot back. "Maybe if Kristal could sleep where she's used to sleeping, we wouldn't have this problem."

"I'm trying to conduct an interview in there!"

"You might have scheduled it around Kristal's nap."

"This is ludicrous—"

"Tell me about it."

"Dammit, Isabel, it can't go on. *Do* something!"

He stalked back to his office and slammed the door.

Isabel glared after him. "All right," she muttered. "I will."

She gathered up her purse, her coat and her daughter, and left.

When she walked into her condo, the phone was ringing. Sure that it was Eric and unwilling to cope with him just then, she ignored it. She fixed Kristal a bottle, gave her some baby medication and put her to bed.

Afterward, dropping her clothes as she went, she sauntered into the living room. She kicked off her shoes—one landed smack on the coffee table—and in her stocking feet walked over to the easel she'd set up in front of the window. On it sat an almost completed portrait of Eric. She'd been painting from memory and thought she'd captured his brooding good looks quite admirably.

She had painted it—and intended to present him with the completed picture—as another way of repaying the debt she felt she owed him. Or so she told Delores. And herself.

Right then, however, furious with him, she only wanted to stick her tongue out at it. At him. She did.

Feeling better, she marched into her bedroom, stripping as she went. She took a quick shower, then slipped into sweats. She had just squeezed dabs of paint onto her palette when someone knocked. Sighing, Isabel went to open the door.

"What do you think you're doing here?" Eric shouldered past her into the small foyer. To hell with friendly and businesslike.

"Won't you come in," Isabel drawled, closing the door behind him. She followed him to the living room archway, remembered the portrait and scooted past him. "Don't go in there."

He stopped to stare at her. "Why not?"

"It-it's a mess."

He shrugged, pointedly eyeing her discarded coat on the floor. "I expected no less."

"Meaning?"

"Meaning it's always a mess, Isabel. My God—" he walked past her into the living room and waved a hand "—how can you live like this?"

"Very well, thank you." She sniffed and gave a toss of her head. She went to the easel, thinking to drape something over the picture before Eric spotted his half-finished likeness. Too late. He was right behind her.

"What's this?"

"None of your business." She yanked up the first piece of cloth her hand touched. It was a skirt she'd worn a couple of days ago. She flung it over the picture.

He took it off, identified what it was with a shake of the head, and dropped it. Then he looked at the picture. "Why, it's me."

Isabel tried to cover her discomfort with sarcasm. "And here I thought it was Elvis Presley." She fiddled with her paints.

"It's very good," Eric marveled.

"So now he's an art critic."

"Were you planning to give it to me, Isabel?"

"No, I thought I'd auction it off," she snapped, tossing the skirt back over it. "You have no right to come marching in here, R. E. Schwenker, barging into my privacy...."

For a moment, enthralled by the painting, Eric had forgotten why he was there. Isabel's outburst reminded him and, at the same time, sparked his own temper.

"As long as you're on company time, you have no privacy," he countered sharply. "How dare you leave in the middle of the day without saying a word?"

"You told me to do something about Kristal," she flung back. "I did. I took her home."

He scowled down at her for long moments, then abruptly turned away.

Isabel crossed her arms and girded herself for further battle. She should have known by now it wouldn't come.

"It's no good, you know," he said very quietly. "Things aren't working out with us the way I thought they would."

His words and the sorrowful tone in which he said them completely disarmed Isabel. Letting her arms drop, she slowly nodded. More and more lately, she'd been thinking the same thing.

"Kristal's growing," Eric went on, keeping his back to her. *I want you all the time,* he thought. *And it's hell being with you and not being able to do anything about that want.* "And even when she's happy and healthy, she's becoming more active and noisy. As kids should be. Except . . ." He shrugged and looked down at his hands.

"Not in a work environment, I know," Isabel said. *Besides,* she thought sadly, *things between you and me can't go on as they have. I'm falling in love with you.*

As if he'd heard her thoughts, he turned to face her. For long heavy moments he looked at her. "What's to be done, Isabel?"

She hung her head. "Nothing," she said in a small voice. "Except to move on."

Move on? Out of his life? Eric didn't want that, but . . . what did he want? He reached for her. "Isabel . . ."

"No, Eric." She shook her head and gave him a lopsided smile. "Don't say anything else. I'll always be grateful for what you've done for me. For us. If only—"

She stopped, another sharp shake of her head negating what she'd been about to say. *If only things were different.* That was her heart talking, not her head. Her head dealt in realities, which in her case meant sticking to the resolutions she'd made after her disastrous marriage had ended: to live her life only for herself and for Kristal.

Lately she'd begun to forget that resolution, and she'd been content to relinquish some control over her life. It had to stop, but it wouldn't as long as she had Eric to lean on.

And so she said, "I'll get my mother to watch Kristal for a few days so I can interview a replacement secretary."

"Thank you."

If only.

Eric, too, was torn by those two little words. He asked himself, If only *what?* If only he were different? Or she? If only she were more in line with his fantasy of the proper wife?

Yeah. He sighed. Something like that.

Chapter Nine

In interviewing secretarial candidates to replace her, Isabel made it a point to be scrupulously unbiased and fair.

Or so she told herself.

The employment agency sent over an impressive string of women—young and not so young, and ranging from magnificent to mousy in looks and demeanor. They also sent one man. Twenty-five, average-looking, pleasant. The skills of the applicants encompassed the spectrum from appalling to admirable. After several days of interviews and tests, Isabel had narrowed the field to three.

The final choice had to be made by Eric, of course. Isabel had insisted on that since he, not she, would have to live with whatever choice was made.

Now, after knocking on Eric's office door, Isabel entered when he bade her to. She noted that he needed a haircut and that he looked tired and drawn. With difficulty, she managed to squelch the urge to comment on either, reminding herself that she had no business worrying about him like that. If she'd wanted that right, she shouldn't have rebuffed his advances the way she had that painful afternoon. It was too late now for regrets.

"I've got the applications and my evaluations here for your review," she said. Handing him the sheaf of papers, she added, "For the three secretarial candidates."

"Oh." Eric slanted her a look from beneath puckered brows, his fingers riffling the pages. "These are the cream of the crop, eh?" He pointed to a chair. "Please have a seat."

"Thank you." Isabel sat down next to his desk and primly folded her hands in her lap. "And, yes, in my judgment these are the most suitable."

"Hmm." Eric scanned the topmost applicant. Smith, Roger A. He looked up, surprised. "He's male!"

Isabel stiffened. "That's correct."

Eric frowned. "We're looking for a *secretary*. Does the man realize—"

"—that the job is *women's* work?" Isabel jumped in, her careful courtesy of the past few days forgotten in the face of this familiar bone of contention. "Apparently not."

Eric gritted his teeth. God, but the woman had a chip on her shoulder at times. He tightened his grip on the application, gave it a snappy shake to straighten it and, with a quelling look at her, continued with what he'd been about to say.

"Does he realize that Schwenker Engineering can't offer him much in the way of advancement? We're a small business...."

"He understands that." Isabel felt foolish for having jumped a gun he'd apparently had no intention of firing. Perversely, though, she felt a bit let down, too. They were always tiptoeing around each other these days....

If Eric's scowling perusal of the application was anything to go by, he wasn't too pleased with her choice. To prod him into voicing a reaction so that she could rebut, she added, "You'll note that Smith earned exceptionally good grades in business school."

"Hmm."

"And that he was at his previous job for three years."

Her tone seemed laced with challenge. Eric slanted her another sharp look. "What made him decide to leave? Or did you ask?"

Isabel bristled. "Of course I asked. It was one of my first questions."

"And?"

"As I recall, he merely wanted a change." She shrugged, trying to seem offhand so that Eric wouldn't see how very much she wanted him to hire Smith. It'd be a real feather in her cap to have converted a diehard chauvinist like R. E. Schwenker to the point of hiring a male for a traditionally female position. Besides, she'd feel much better knowing some cute young thing wasn't—

She stopped herself just in time, sternly told herself such petty considerations had not been part of her rationale in the least. The fact that the two female finalists she'd come up with were middle-aged was purely coincidental.

"People do make changes, you know."

"Yes. I know."

Isabel fidgeted beneath his suddenly brooding stare. She was sure he wasn't thinking of Smith just then, and his next words confirmed it.

"Will you be happy with the changes you're making, Isabel?"

She blinked. She'd asked herself that often over the past few days, only to quickly remind herself she wasn't *making* changes so much as *un*making those that had occurred without conscious input from her. She'd been swept along on Eric Schwenker's wave of goodwill for a while and now it was time to swim on her own again. Or at least practically on her own.

She forced a bright smile. "Of course I'll be happy. I, that is Kristal and I, will be moving to Bellingham, you know. With my mother."

Eric blanched. "You're what?"

"I said—"

"I heard what you said." Appalled by her announcement, and even more so by the almost physical pain it caused him, he surged to his feet. "Had you planned to tell me about it, or did you intend just to send me a change-of-address notice?"

Isabel shrank back in her chair, away from him and his almost threatening stance. Noting the small movement, Eric stifled a curse and sat back down. He forced a more moderate tone.

"When did this decision come about?"

Isabel shrugged, eyeing him warily because she'd never seen Eric come so close to losing control. He'd been angry, no, outraged by her words. Why? They'd already decided to part company, hadn't they? What did it matter where she went?

"My mother needs us," she said. "And I need her, too. I don't want to put Kristal into day care—"

"Heaven forbid."

"—and Delly is glad to look after her. She's lonely."

Eric was getting to know loneliness himself pretty well these days. He stared at his desk, then slowly lifted his eyes to Isabel's. "I'm going to miss you, you know."

Isabel swallowed. "I was leaving anyway, remember?"

"I remember." Eric heaved a sigh. "But I thought, I'd hoped... Never mind." He'd thought he'd see her—

them—from time to time. The move to Bellingham, though only about eighty miles across the border, seemed to take her irrevocably out of his reach.

"Do you plan to get a job down there?" he asked, more to bridge the lengthening silence than out of real curiosity. She was going away. He really couldn't think beyond that. "If you need references..."

"No. But thanks." Isabel smiled at him. When he didn't smile back, she cleared her throat and added, "I'm planning to go back to school."

"Oh?"

"Western Washington State University is there, you know."

"Oh, yes." Were they really having this innocuous conversation? "Any special major?"

"Art," Isabel said. "Delly looked at my paintings. She thinks I have talent."

"You do." Eric said it warmly, sincerely. He thought, *And so much more.* She had so much to offer... someone. Just then he wished that someone could be him. He couldn't seem to remember why that wasn't possible. Had he been the one to put the brakes on their burgeoning attraction, or had it been she? No matter now, she had made her plans and they didn't include him. Or any other man. That thought made him feel better, though not much. Just enough to remind him that the least he could do for her was seem supportive.

"I wish you all the very best, Isabel," he said quietly. "You know that, don't you?"

She nodded. "Yes."

They studied each other. Eric noted a sheen of tears in Isabel's eyes and, knowing how she despised showing weakness, thought it best to get away from the personal as quickly as possible.

"So," he said, forcing a brisk tone and making a project out of picking up the applications again, "where were we?"

"Roger Smith," Isabel murmured after a moment's hesitation during which she struggled to mask the hurt she felt at his abrupt switch back to business. She must have been wrong earlier to think her announcement would upset him; he'd probably only been angry because she hadn't told him of her plans before now.

Hurt escalated quickly into resentment. The decision to move in with Delores had been a difficult one to make. She'd spent several sleepless nights struggling to come to grips with the fact that once she moved away from Vancouver she'd probably never see Eric again.

And here it was obvious he wouldn't be losing any sleep over it.

"You'll recall we were discussing his reasons for leaving his previous job," she said with a sniff.

"Ahh, yes." Eric showed no emotion as he carefully laid Smith's application aside and picked up the next.

Isabel bit her lip, wanting to be every bit as cool as he was being, but the words tumbled out of her mouth in spite of herself. "You yourself said things couldn't go on with us as they had."

"I know. And it's all right." Eric glanced at her. Isabel looked as upset as he felt. Confrontations, though she never backed away from them, made her uneasy, he reminded himself. She probably thought he was angry. He forced a smile of reassurance, but, dammit, he *was* angry. How could she simply pack up and move when he—

Feeling his blood pressure soar, he instantly put the brakes on whatever he was thinking. After all, what right did he have to expect anything of Isabel? She owed him nothing; he'd said so himself more than once. And it was true. Yet...

Impatient with himself, he made an effort to concentrate on the matter at hand. Isabel's damn replacement. Grimly, he read the application. Name: Lefkovitz, Anita C. She seemed to have quite a lot of experience. "Isabel, just how old is Ms. Lefkovitz?"

"Fifty."

"Fifty!" He didn't want to react, but something had to give or he'd burst, so it might as well be this.

Fighting words, and with hurt and resentment still almost choking her, just what Isabel needed. "First it's gender, now it's age," she flared. "Are you so superficial you don't care about such things as experience and references?"

"I care as much as the next guy—"

"Ha!" Isabel was on her feet and leaning halfway across his desk. "You, R. E. Schwenker, are the biggest chauvinist that ever walked this earth. You've got things all figured out, haven't you, about who does what and where to whom, and woe are they who don't fit your mold. Well, I've got news for you—"

"Oh, really?" Eric was on his feet, too, and every bit as furious as Isabel. "I'd watch who I call a chauvinist, *Ms.* Mott, because people in glass houses shouldn't be tossing rocks around—"

"Meaning?"

"Meaning just because of one bad apple you go around condemning the whole damn barrel. Meaning you're so afraid of being vulnerable, you won't allow yourself to be a woman. Meaning you don't think women should be equal to men—they should be better."

Staring into her set face, he felt the fire abruptly go out of him. "Just because a man wants to take care of a woman and, in turn, have her take care of him, doesn't mean he wants to dominate and diminish her, Isabel.''

"Doesn't it?" Isabel blustered, but the urge to fight had left her, too. "Says you," she said wearily and straightened away from the desk.

She glanced down at her hands, balled into fists on the edge of it. She squeezed her eyes shut and sucked in a shuddering breath.

"I think I'd better leave, Eric," she said hoarsely. "Right away. There's nothing left for me to do here." She nodded blindly toward the applications. "Any of those three can come and take over here at a moment's notice."

"I see." Eric felt as if he'd been punched in the gut. His breath seemed to have gotten stuck somewhere. It struggled past his throat with something that sounded embarrassingly like a quaver. He clamped his teeth together and sat down.

Isabel waited for him to say something else, something that showed he cared as much, hurt as much, as she did. But he said nothing, and so, without looking at him again, she choked out a goodbye and left the room.

Had his life been this humdrum before Isabel Mott and her child had made their brief appearance in it? Eric wondered, driving home from the Sloanses' place in West Vancouver. He didn't think so, yet he couldn't seem to recapture whatever ingredient had added the spark that was missing these days. Now, as then, he went to work, played indoor tennis, went up Grouse Mountain or drove to Whistler for some late-spring skiing. He had no desire to date. None of the women he knew or met were anything special. They were attractive, ambitious, bright.

And, compared to Isabel, somehow lacking.

Dinner tonight with Mike and Sunny Sloan hadn't helped to alleviate this nagging discontent, though he'd hope it would. Always before, observing the chaos that was the Sloan household had reinforced his own conviction that for a man to tie himself to a free-thinking career woman was pure and simply folly. Though he was tremendously fond of Mike, there had always been a tiny part of himself that pitied the poor sap—a brilliant physician, for heaven's sake—for allowing himself to be roped into doing such mundane domestic tasks as washing laundry and dishes, and dusting the furniture.

Mike, well aware of Eric's unvoiced disapproval, would only laugh, saying, "Just you wait, old buddy. Your turn will come." But, of course, Eric had known better. If and when he married there'd be strict division of labor, all right, but not in the way of the Sloans. No sir. In his marriage he, the husband, would work at his job to provide the home that his wife would manage. Alone. It was as simple as that.

Or at least it used to be.

God help him, but this time, watching Mike labor in the kitchen alongside his wife, Eric had felt none of his usual pitying superiority. Instead, there had been a niggling sense of—he had no other word for the unwelcome emotion— envy. Mike and Sunny were perfectly happy, working as a team to put the meal together. They joked and bantered, bumping into each other, even stopping to kiss. They chatted about their respective days—Sunny was an X-ray technician—laughed a lot and did some touching as she made salad and he his "famous" marinara sauce.

They'd put Eric in charge of keeping an eye on the bubbling pasta. But when he kept letting the water boil over, they figuratively patted him on the head, pressed a glass of

Chianti into his hand and told him to sit somewhere out of the way.

He felt like a bumbling fool, inept. And again, envious of Mike's domestic skills and wedded bliss.

Dinner had begun like an inquisition and ended like a wake.

"So, how're things with you and the beauteous *secretary?*" Mike asked with an exaggerated wink at Sunny. "We thought you'd bring her with you tonight, old bud."

"Yes, Rudy," Sunny seconded, pressing more sauce on him. "Why didn't you? She could've brought the baby along if a sitter was the problem."

"In fact, Sunny was looking forward to the little girl," Mike offered with a fond pat on his wife's bulging midriff. "Sort of as practice for the one we have in there."

"Then you're sure now it's a girl?" Eric grabbed the chance to steer the conversation away from himself. He didn't care to discuss Isabel with anyone, not even his closest friends. After all, what was there to say? She was gone.

"Yep. Had the ultrasound." Mike beamed. "We're making you a god*mother,* buddy. Get it?" He chortled delightedly at his own humor while Sunny and Eric exchanged oh-brother looks.

"God, you're corny." Sunny rolled her eyes, then turned back to Eric. "You know, we still can't agree on a name for her. Isn't that awful? All we know is we don't want one from either side of the family because there's bound to be hurt feelings unless we give the poor kid a whole string of middle names. What's your little girl called?"

Your little girl. Eric couldn't believe how good that sounded and how much he found himself wishing Kristal really had been his. "Kristal is hardly my little girl, Sunny."

"You know what I mean." Sunny dismissed his objection with a wave of her fork. "Kristal," she mused. "That's kind of pretty. Kristal Sloan..." Screwing up her face, she listened to the sound of it, then grimaced. "Naw." She twirled her spaghetti. "Together with Sloan, it lacks a certain ring, you know? What's your Kristal's last name?"

"She's not *my* Kristal, all right?" Suddenly Eric had had it—watching the Sloanses' domestic idyll, their talk of babies and names. Everything. Dropping his fork, he yanked his napkin off his lap and tossed it down, too. "Look, excuse me, but I've got to go."

Scraping back his chair and already half out of it, he took in his hosts' shocked and bewildered expressions. With a strangled sort of groan, he collapsed back down. "God, I'm sorry...."

"So am I," Sunny said quietly. She touched his arm. "I keep going on and on.... Something's wrong, Rudy, isn't it?"

Yeah, Eric thought disgustedly. Something's wrong, all right. The trouble was, if things were so damn *wrong* now, shouldn't it follow they'd been *right* before? Yet they hadn't been, had they?

"Hell, I don't know." He scrubbed a hand across his face, then let it drop. He slanted Sunny a sideways glance of apology. "All I know is I'm being a rotten guest and you guys don't deserve that."

"Bull," Mike said with finality. "We're your friends. If you're feeling rotten, this is the place to let it all hang out. We're on your side, old buddy."

"I know." Eric sighed. "Trouble is, I don't know which side I'm on myself anymore."

"What the hell does that mean?"

Eric pushed back his chair and stood up. "Damned if I know."

But he did know. Deep down at gut level, Eric knew exactly which side he was on and why things felt wrong. But he didn't like what he knew, and so he told himself that before Isabel and her little girl had rolled into his life—and yes, dammit, into his heart—he'd been a contented man. The sun, moon and stars were in the sky; God was in His heaven. Right was right and wrong was wrong, and he'd never doubted which was which.

Enter Isabel, exit peace of mind. Enter doubt.

Just as the constant drip, drip, drip of water on rock eventually blunted its edges and changed its shape, so had his association with Isabel gradually eroded and changed the substance and foundation of his value system. As a result, beliefs that once had seemed clear-cut and unshakable were now no longer either.

He was wallowing in uncertainty and it was driving him crazy.

In the sleepless night following his dinner with the Sloans, he finally decided that enough was enough. Being by nature logical and by training methodical, he forced himself to dissect the problem and examine his options, which brought him to the conclusion that the only way he could get himself back on track was to return to square one. Back to his beginnings. Back to the place and the people who had instilled in him the values he'd believed immutable—until Isabel Mott had made him doubt.

It was time to reaffirm his values. And who knew? Maybe while he was at it, he'd find the kind of wife he'd been looking for, too.

You can never go back.

Eric had no idea where he'd heard or read that statement, or who the author was, but he quickly came to appreciate its veracity. He had returned to the country of his birth expecting things to have remained unchanged in the near dozen years of his absence, but of course they hadn't. In fact, very little of his tiny hometown looked as he remembered it—the streets seemed narrower, the houses shabbier, the people less friendly. His friends had aged much more than he, it seemed, and they'd become stodgy, opinionated, narrow-minded. Everything was different.

Or could it be he was the one who was different?

He fought the truth of that at first, but eventually had to concede that, yes, he had indeed changed. He no longer fit in, no longer belonged. Also—and this was the most difficult discovery for Eric to come to terms with—he could no longer accept the very status quo he'd come to reaffirm.

He found he hated to sit with the men, drinking and talking and playing cards, while their wives—his sisters, his mother, their friends—scurried hither and yon, waiting on them like so many slaves. His efforts to make them sit down, to draw them into the conversation, met with embarrassed reluctance on the part of the women and hostile silence on the part of the men. In moments the pointed stares from their spouses would have the women back up on their feet.

Eric had been taken aside by his father and reminded that in this town, at least, women still knew their place and that people liked to keep things that way. This little lecture was typical of his father, who considered it his prerogative to meddle in the life of every member of his family. It had gone a long way toward convincing Eric that coming home—coming back and trying to recapture the past—was not possible.

Not only did the man he had become resent his father's dictatorial stance, he questioned his father's right to assume it. It took considerable self-control for Eric not to reply with words that would have been deemed disrespectful and that would have created a scene. He'd bitten his tongue and walked away.

Everything came to a head for him during a visit with his older sister, Magda. She was closest to him in age, and as children they'd been the best of friends. Eric was grateful to find that closeness unchanged.

Magda was newly married and employed as a nursery-school teacher. She was the only female member of his family who had continued at her job after the wedding, a fact that caused much clucking of tongues. Magda staunchly stuck to her guns.

"Of course Jon and I want a family some day," she confided, "but we want other things first. A telephone, a washing machine, perhaps a car and the chance to travel a little. Why is that so wrong?"

"It isn't," Eric assured her.

"Then why does everyone act as if I'm staging a revolution by not staying home and having babies right away?"

Eric pulled a wry face. "Traditions?"

"Hmm." Magda sighed. "I agree they're important, but..."

They were alone in the tiny, immaculately clean apartment Magda and her husband, Jonathan, had been lucky to get. Jon was away, working the evening shift in a manufacturing plant some miles out of town. Magda was serving Eric coffee and cake in spite of his protests.

"I don't want anything but your company for a change!" he exclaimed, attempting to drag her down onto the sofa beside him. "Sit, will you?"

"But I'm so happy to have you here I just want to spoil you a little while I can," she countered, pressing another slice of crumb cake on him. "You're too thin, Eric. Doesn't anyone feed you over there?"

But she did sit down eventually and even drank coffee with him, which Eric considered a real coup. They talked, sort of, with Magda asking questions that Eric did his utmost to answer as fully as he could. His sister was spellbound by his tales of the United States and Canada and of the life he had found there.

She wanted to hear every detail, especially as it related to the current fashions and to the ways the women there were different from her and her peers.

"Is it true that they're as bold as men?" she asked in a voice that was tinged with traces of contempt, as well as a generous dose of envy. "And that they dye their hair and paint their faces, and speak their mind uninvited on any subject?"

Eric laughed. "Oh, yes."

Unbidden, but inevitably, Isabel's image popped onto his mental screen. And though thinking of her caused a stab of pain and regret, he couldn't help but chuckle in fond reminiscence of the many and lively set-tos they'd had.

"They speak their minds, all right," he conceded. "But as to the rest of it—" he shrugged "—some women wear more makeup than others—it really depends on the occasion or on the work they do. A salesclerk or a secretary or a model will act and look differently from someone who...well, drives a truck, for instance."

"Drives a truck?" Magda gaped, wide-eyed.

"Well, yes," Eric defended, piqued by what he perceived to be a shocked reaction. It was one thing for him to find fault with some of the customs of his adopted homeland, quite another for an outsider to dare to do the same. "Women are every bit as capable as men, you know."

"Yes, I know," Magda said quietly, surprising him. "It's unexpected to hear that you know it, too, though. You've changed, Eric."

His responding frown made her smile. "Knowing how much like Papa you always were, I gather those changes haven't been easy to make or accept." She shyly touched his hand. "You say you are happy in your new country, little brother, yet all these days you've looked troubled more often than not."

Eric stiffened. "Just because I don't go around smiling all the time—"

"No, no," Magda interrupted. "That's not your way, I know that. But there are shadows in your eyes—"

"Jet lag," he said curtly. "I'm tired."

"Of course." She backed off instantly, as she'd been taught to do when a man made it clear he didn't care to pursue a topic. For a short while, she'd forgotten herself and her place.

Noticing her withdrawal, Eric roundly cursed himself. Here he'd finally managed to draw her out, to get her to talk to him as an equal, and then he'd sent her back into her shell with his damned attitude.

"If I seem unhappy," he said reluctantly, uncomfortable about baring his soul even a little, "it's because I'd very much like to settle down and have a family, but I seem to have lost sight of what's important somewhere along the line. I thought I might find it here, but . . ."

He shrugged, frowning at some elusive thought teasing the edge of his mind.

His sister watched him with obvious incomprehension.

"I came back here thinking I might find the right woman," he elaborated absently—and then it hit him, that elusive thought, right between the eyes.

There was no woman who was right for him here. How could there be? The woman for him lived thousands of miles away in a small city called Bellingham, in Washington state.

Good Lord. He stared at Magda, feeling as though someone had yanked a blindfold off his eyes and now he could see.

The right woman for him was Isabel Mott. It was so clear, suddenly, so simple. He loved her. And though she might not know it yet, she loved him, too.

So what if she was assertive, independent, a lousy cook and a worse housekeeper? She was organized and efficient when it came to running a business. She was a most devoted mother. She had courage, she had wit. She had glorious green eyes a man could drown in, and lips that were satin soft and honey sweet.

He wanted her, but more than that, he loved her.

It was all he could do to stay in his seat as the truth struck him like summer lightning and sent electrifying energy surging through his limbs. He wanted to leap off the couch, rush to the nearest airport and hijack the first plane out of there.

He wanted to go home. Home to Isabel.

He sat in amazement. How could he have been so stupid? How could he have just let her walk out of his life? How could he not have realized... He laughed, a short bark of a laugh that expressed self-derision rather than mirth.

"What an idiot I've been," he said, astounding his sister further. "But I guess it took this trip to make that clear to me."

"Eric. I don't understand..."

"Neither did I, sweetheart." Eric leaned over and impulsively kissed her smack on the mouth. "Oh, but I do now!"

The sun was shining. It had to be, because Isabel could feel its heat on her bare arms and legs, and on the back of her neck. But to her the world—the trees, the mountains, and the sea at which she was joylessly staring—was lackluster and gray. Everything seemed as devoid of color as the charcoal sketch she was supposed to be making, but for which she couldn't work up even a shred of enthusiasm.

She didn't feel like sketching any more than she felt like painting, or attending classes, or eating, or even playing with Kristal. All she felt like doing these days was sleeping. In the morning it took a major effort to drag herself out of bed, and most nights she was back in it just as soon as Kristal had been put in hers. Then she'd stick her head beneath the pillow to shut out any light and noise, and she'd will herself into oblivion until—always too soon— the relentless jangle of the alarm harangued her to reluctant consciousness once again.

Depression had been Doc Kramer's diagnosis when a worried Delores had coerced Isabel into his office. He'd prescribed some pills to help lift her spirits, and lots of exercise in the fresh air. Isabel stubbornly refused to take the pills, but his other advice had her daily roaming the countryside in good weather or foul. And though she always took along her artist's paraphernalia, she was blind to the beauty that surrounded her.

Which didn't matter, since every sketch she attempted, regardless of the subject, yielded the same uninspired result. Whereupon she'd tear it off the pad and rip it to shreds.

Today was no different. Except that when she went to destroy her drawing in exasperated fury, a veined and increasingly gnarled hand reached across her shoulder and held the paper in place.

"So that's what you draw when you sit around staring day after day," Delores said after a lengthy interval of silent study during which Isabel sat as if carved from stone. "It's a pretty decent likeness of the man, at that."

"Where's Kristal?"

"She's exhausted from chasing butterflies, and so am I." Delores gingerly lowered herself onto a boulder next to Isabel. "Since that child learned to walk, I swear I've lost ten pounds. Now she's asleep on the blanket over there in the shade."

"I think I'll go join her." Isabel tossed her sketchbook aside and made to rise, but again her mother's hand stayed her.

"It's time we talked about what's bothering you."

"Mo-*ther*..."

"No." The hint of steel had been absent from Delores's tone for many years, but it instantly reminded Isabel of those childhood days when she'd made a career out of stretching her mother's patience to the limit. Any minute now sparks would fly.

Since she didn't have the energy just then to deal with her mother's wrath, she subsided back onto the ground with a resigned sigh. Staring moodily into the distance, she said, "So talk."

"You cannot go on like this, Isabel. I won't have it."

That brought a reaction. Isabel's head whipped around. She gaped at her mother. "*You* won't have it?"

"That's right," Delores said sternly. "And you needn't look so outraged. It's bad enough that you're neglecting yourself, your studies and your art—I told myself it's your life and that you need to deal with your problems in your own way and time—but when you begin to neglect your child—"

"How have I done that?" Isabel flared, roused from her lethargy by her mother's charge. "Isn't she here with me this very moment? Don't I take her everywhere?"

"In body, yes, but not in spirit."

"Well, you're a fine one to talk, aren't you?" Something snapped inside Isabel. She'd kept too many emotions bottled up lately. "I never even had you in body when I was growing up, did I? I was always shunted off to Grandma Abby's—"

"Stop it," Delores cut in sharply. "We've dealt with that and it's done. It's time to stop feeling sorry for yourself, Isabel. Time to take responsibility for your life without always looking for blame in the past. Your unhappiness now has nothing to do with me, or even with—"

"Oh, sure," Isabel bitterly interrupted. "I'm in love with a man and I can't bring myself to let him know it, to make a commitment, because you and Dad were such shining examples of married bliss."

"That isn't why and you know it." Delores caught Isabel's chin in her hand. "Isabel, look at me."

Reluctantly, Isabel complied.

Delores took in the mulish set of her daughter's mouth and the defiant glint in her emerald eyes. A fond smile lit her face. "Right now you look just like Kristal," she said tenderly, "when she doesn't want to eat what's good for her."

Isabel's expression didn't soften.

"But," Delores continued undeterred, "just as Kristal has to swallow what I feed her, so you have to listen to what I have to say. Isabel, the bottom line is you once made a bad choice and now you're scared. Period."

Isabel jerked free of her mother's hand and averted her eyes. "I am not."

"You are," Delores contradicted firmly. "And that's perfectly understandable. Emotional bruises fade much more slowly than those that show on your body. But in order to heal, they need help from yourself and from those you love and trust. If you think Eric Schwenker is that man..."

Delores waited for Isabel to react, to look at her. When she continued to just sit there, staring into the distance, her voice softened. "I know whereof I speak, sweetheart."

"You?" Isabel's head whipped around again. "What do you mean?"

"Marcus Kramer. He was there when the bottom fell out of my life, and even though I struggled against what he was offering, just as you are struggling, he stuck around until I realized how much I needed him."

"Yes, well." Isabel swallowed. "You don't exactly see Eric Schwenker hanging around here, though, do you?"

"No," Delores conceded, "I don't. On the other hand, have you ever given him any reason to think you'd want him to?"

Isabel thoughtfully returned her mother's expectant gaze. They looked at each other in silence for long moments before Delores prompted, "You *do* want him to, don't you?"

Isabel closed her eyes and slowly nodded. "Yes." She slumped forward, her chin dropping to her chest. "Oh, God, yes."

"Then what're you waiting for, girl?" her mother exclaimed with a catch in her voice. "Go and tell the man so."

Chapter Ten

Eric got back to Vancouver on Tuesday, and though he longed to simply get in the car and continue on to Bellingham right then and there, he reluctantly restrained himself. He'd been gone from his business for nearly three weeks, and no doubt a stack of stuff was in dire need of his attention.

"Morning, Roger," he greeted his secretary, striding into the office Wednesday morning. "What've you got for me?"

"Well, hello!" Smith swiveled away from the computer screen to beam at his boss. "You're back early. Didn't think we could hack it without you, is that it?"

"By now I should know better, shouldn't I?" Eric laughed. "Between you running the office, Skip Morrison doing most of the designs and Frank cracking the whip in the shop, I've become completely expendable."

Chalk up one more point for Isabel, Eric thought, surveying the secretary's well-ordered office. Roger Smith was the best thing that ever happened to Schwenker Engineering, and Eric had long since admitted to himself that he'd been wrong to ever have had reservations about hiring the man.

"Well, now, I wouldn't exactly say expendable," Smith countered smartly. "Granted Skip's a great engineer, and Frank and I each do our jobs pretty well, but we'd never get along without you entirely, boss."

"Oh?" Eric, looking skeptical, waited for the other shoe to drop.

Seeing his expression, Smith laughed. Tongue-in-cheek, he added, "We still need your John Hancock on the old paycheck, you know."

"Ha!" Eric moved toward his office, shaking his head. At the door he stopped to send his grinning secretary an arch look. "And you can bet I'll make damn sure it stays that way."

He worked with barely a break, and even took stuff home at night. By Friday noon, he'd had it. The sun shone out of a brilliant sky, birds twittered and cheeped outside the open window. A mellow early-summer breeze stroked his cheeks and riffled his papers. Abruptly, Eric gave up trying to resist the urgings of his heart. He tossed down his pen, grabbed his jacket and, slinging it over one shoulder, headed for the door.

"Think I'll knock off early," he informed his secretary on the way out. "Do some hunting down south."

"Hunting?" Roger stared at the already closing door. "But it's the wrong season."

The door opened again to briefly reveal R. E. Schwenker's wolfish grin. "That's what you think."

The freeway heading south was already clogged with traffic. Not surprisingly for a warm and sunny Friday afternoon, there were many who were anxious to get an early start on their weekend. Bellingham and, some eighty miles farther down the road, Seattle, were popular shopping destinations for the people of British Columbia's lower mainland.

Shopping, however, was the furthest thing from Eric Schwenker's mind. So was hunting.

His earlier cocky stance had long since been blasted to smithereens by the volley of self-doubt with which he'd been bombarding himself. And so now his thoughts were centered squarely on Isabel Mott and the many arguments she would no doubt offer in response to the proposal of marriage Eric intended to make. Even in the unlikely event she agreed to marry him, she'd have arguments first, of this Eric was sure.

Inching his way forward in the long slow line approaching the Canada-U.S. border, he kept himself from going crazy by trying to think up rebuttals to every objection she might possibly raise.

If she said, "But I don't love you," he'd say he didn't believe her.

If she said, "It'll never work," he'd say, yes, it would.

If she said, "But I don't want to get married again," he'd say, yes, she did.

If she said— He snorted in disgust. This was ludicrous.

While his foot eased off the brake, allowing the car to creep ahead another couple of feet, his mind jeered that if those pitiful rebuttals were the best he could come up with, he might as well pack it in right there and then.

He ground his teeth in frustration. Eloquence had never been his strong suit. He'd always been a terrible debater. Words were not his forte; numbers were. One and one makes two. He smiled in spite of his worries. And Kristal makes three.

He sighed. Numbers didn't lie, but words did. Yet he'd better have all the eloquence of a seasoned politician if he wanted to convince Isabel that she needed him as much as he needed her.

What made him think he had a chance? What made him think she might possibly be in love with him? Her responsiveness to his kiss? He'd caught her by surprise that time, and she'd made very sure there'd been no repeat.

Then what about those small glimpses of jealousy he thought he'd caught from time to time?

Ha!

Since when was he such a wonderful judge of reactions and character? He'd thought that Jones woman a suitable secretary, too, hadn't he?

If at that point there had been an opportunity to get out of line and turn the car around, Eric would have done so. Panic squeezed his heart like a vise as he realized that there was no way he'd be able to persuade Isabel Mott to see his point of view if she didn't want to be persuaded. And why should she want to be? She'd done just fine on her own until now....

By the time he was waved on his way by the customs-and-immigration officer, Eric was calling himself all manner of fool. But he drove on regardless.

In Bellingham he only had to ask directions once. Everyone seemed to know Delores Kant, the famous watercolor artist. She was, after all, one of the city's most prominent citizens. Eric hadn't expected the house in which she lived to be so unassuming; he had, to be honest, not spared the place a thought at all until he drove up to it. Its age and simplicity surprised him—it was hardly more than a cottage.

About to press the doorbell, he spotted a small note tacked on the wall next to it. "Please don't ring, knock. Baby sleeping."

Still? He checked his watch—three-thirty. If Kristal had been this good a napper when her mother was still in his employ, things might be different now.

Sucking in a deep breath, he knocked. Once, and then once again, a little more forcefully. Footsteps. His heart did a calypso-drum imitation against his rib cage. He squared his shoulders and drew in another long breath, which was unnervingly shaky. As the door was flung wide, he cleared his throat, because it had chosen that moment to close up.

Delores Kant, dressed in a paint-smeared smock over faded jeans, peered myopically up at him with polite inquiry.

Eric released the breath he'd unconsciously held in a loud rush of disappointment. "Hello."

"Hel-*lo!*" Surprised recognition had Delores's voice rise a few notes on the second syllable. She reached for his hand, eagerly tugged him inside. "Come in, come in."

"Well . . . thank you. I—"

"Why, this is terrific," Delores gushed, apparently unaware that she was astounding her guest not a little with her welcome. "It's so good to see you. Isn't it good to see him, dear?" she called over her shoulder, causing Eric to swing his gaze in that direction, expecting to see Isabel.

A bearded man, almost a head taller than Eric, emerged from a doorway with a sleepy-eyed Kristal in his arms. He, too, beamed at Eric.

"This is my dear friend, Dr. Marcus Kramer," Delores said. "Marc, meet Isabel's . . . Meet Eric Schwenker."

"Real good to know you, Schwenker," said the doctor, extending his free hand.

"Please call me Eric." About to shake the offered hand, Eric found he needed both of his own to catch the small body hurling itself at him with squeals of delight. He caught the little girl and swung her high in the air. "Hello, pretty Kristal..."

She stretched her arms down toward him and wiggled in his hands until he lowered her to chest level. Then she hugged his neck with all the strength of a loving boa constrictor and, after kissing him wetly on the mouth, pressed her cheek to his. "Da-da," she said. "Da-da..."

Eric was too involved and too choked up with emotion to notice the quick exchange of looks between Delores and Marcus Kramer. "She calls all of us that," Delores hastened to explain. "Please don't think—"

"That's all right," Eric assured her. "I'm here to convince your daughter that this little darling's daddy is exactly what I need to become."

"Oh. Oh, my..." Delores tossed Marcus an ecstatic smile. "Did you hear that, Marc? He came to convince Isabel..."

Marcus gently patted her shoulder and winked at Eric. "I heard, Delly. And maybe we ought to give the boy a chance to do that then, hmm? Why don't you take the baby and give her a snack, and I'll tell him where to find the woman he's looking for..."

Short minutes later, Eric was back in his car and heading out toward scenic Chuckanut Drive. Isabel was out sketching nature for a class assignment, Marcus had told him. Then, with a clap on the shoulder and another, "Real good to meet you, boy," he'd fairly shoved Eric out the door.

Strange man, Eric mused, then dismissed the good doctor from his mind as he spotted the light blue subcompact he knew to be Isabel's. It was parked along the side of the road beneath a sprawling madrona tree. He pulled onto the shoulder ahead of it, his heart beginning to drum again before he'd even killed the engine.

What was he still worried about? he scoffed as he got out of the car and squinted up the hill where he supposed Isabel was sketching. Would her mother have greeted him as warmly as she had if Isabel hadn't spoken favorably of him? She had to at least *like* him, which was a start....

He set out up the steep path, and soon his shortness of breath and rapid beat of his heart no longer had anything to do with nerves. This was quite a hike. When had he gotten so out of shape?

Damn, it was hot. He stopped to mop his brow and began to pull his sweater off over his head. That's when he saw her. The sweater stayed where it was; his arms dropped back to his sides.

Isabel was in profile to him, perched on a boulder. She was facing seaward, her face tilted up to the sun. Both arms were planted behind her on the rock to support her arched torso. She wore khaki walking shorts that left the golden length of her legs exposed from knee to shapely ankle. A pink tank top left her arms and the graceful column of her throat equally bare. The posture she'd assumed thrust her breasts proudly upward....

Eric's breath caught as his blood quickened. Around him bird song ceased, insects stopped their busy buzz, the entire world shrank to just one thing—Isabel.

With her hair loose and flowing in the gentle breeze, she looked like a siren. The Lorelei must have appeared thus to the unwary sailors on the Rhine, Eric supposed, and began to move toward her, as inexorably drawn as legend had those sailors. Except that when he reached this siren, he didn't plan to die. He planned to live, really live again for the first time in months.

And, with luck, happily ever after.

Gravel crunched beneath his feet. A pebble was kicked ahead a few steps, ricocheted against a rock and bounced down the hill. At the slight noise, Isabel's head whipped around. She stared at him, startled, her expression one of alarm.

Eric stopped walking. The birds and the bees went on about their business in noisy concert. The spell of enchantment that the vision of the rock had cast over him had been broken, but the feeling of wonder lingered in his heart.

It took a moment for Isabel to realize who the tall dark-haired intruder in jeans and light blue cotton sweater was. When she did, she gasped. "Eric."

She swung off the boulder in one lithe move. She began to run to him, then abruptly stopped as the full impact of the situation hit home.

Eric had come to her. She'd been thinking of him just then, daydreaming, planning. And now there he was, as if conjured up by her longings. She drank him in with her eyes, hungrily searched his face. His still, shuttered face.

She took a halting step toward him, then another, her gaze now meshed with his as she tried to gauge what he was thinking, feeling. Why did he look so wary? As if he wasn't sure of his welcome? And then it hit her. He didn't know. He had no way of knowing that in just one more day she would have come to him.

She stopped again. She offered him a smile, putting into it all the love for him that was in her heart. She held both hands out to him in mute invitation.

Eric needed no other encouragement.

He disposed of the space between them with four long strides, and when they were toe-to-toe, he wordlessly pulled her into his arms and covered her mouth with his.

It was a kiss of greeting, of welcome. It was a declaration of love, a staking of claim. It was a promise of ever after.

Isabel rose on tiptoe and wound her arms around Eric's neck in a gesture that was possessive even as she offered herself to be possessed. She fitted her body to his and almost purred her delight. She'd known this was how he'd feel; she remembered it. He was solid and real, yet as exciting as her wildest fantasy. Hot, strong. Hers.

Eric kissed her like the starving man he was; insatiably, he devoured her mouth and always she was there, offering more. So giving, so generous. So soft, sweet, yet full of strength and passion. His Isabel.

He caressed the supple curves of her back, his hands lingering to stroke her derriere before cupping her bottom to forcefully bring her more closely to his hungering body. It wasn't enough, could never be enough until that moment when they were truly one. How he longed for that moment, and Isabel longed for it, too. Every movement, every touch of her body, her hands, her lips, made it clear to him just how much.

The knowledge thrilled him and fueled his passion. If he were to claim her now, he knew she wouldn't stop him. On the contrary, she would welcome him, match him need for need, gift for gift. But dazed and hungering though he was, he knew the time was not yet.

Slowly, their many small sighs and tiny kisses evidence of their reluctance to have the moment end, Isabel and Eric drew apart. Not far, never again far. Just far enough so that they could look into each other's eyes and see reflected there the feelings they had already so eloquently expressed.

"I had geared myself up for a lengthy debate, you know," Eric whispered huskily.

Isabel's gaze shifted to the lopsided grin pulling down one corner of the mouth she'd just so thoroughly kissed. "You had?" she murmured, and quickly kissed it again.

"Hmm." Not about to be outdone, Eric, too, stole several more nibbles of her delectable lips. "I love you," he said when their eyes once again met.

Isabel's hands unclasped from behind Eric's neck to settle on each side of his face, framing it as, without hesitation, she said the words he'd wished so fervently to hear. "And I love you."

Emotion choked him. "I want to marry you, Isabel."

"Sounds good." She stroked her thumbs across his cheeks and marveled at the feel of them—here rough, there smooth. She reveled in the knowledge that he liked what she was doing, and that from now on she could touch him where she wished, when she wished and as often as she wished.

The ease with which Isabel gave her agreement stunned Eric. He'd expected arguments, reservations, if not downright resistance. "It-it does?" he spluttered.

"Oh, yes." For a moment her smile rivaled the radiance of the sun overhead, then it turned mischievous. "Subject to some terms and conditions, of course."

"Aha!" Eric let his hands slide over her torso in one long smooth caress that sent shivers up Isabel's spine. "I knew this victory was too easy."

His thumbs skimmed the sides of her breasts, making him long to linger there, to investigate further. But he didn't. He resolutely forced his hands past temptation and up her arms till they covered the hands still framing his face. Gently, he pulled them down. "Let's walk a little."

Hand in hand, hips and thighs bumping from time to time as they traversed the hilly meadow, they meandered along in silence. Each was content just to know the other was there. They would talk...in time, but for now they inhaled the pine and saltwater-scented air, listened to the concert staged by birds and bees and crickets, and let the wind fan their faces. A soft grassy spot beckoned and in unspoken agreement they dropped onto it.

With a long heartfelt sigh of contentment, Isabel stretched out on her back. Eric lay down next to her on his side, one leg cocked, one elbow propped on the ground to provide support for his head.

Isabel lay with her eyes closed, her arms folded beneath her head, pillowing it. "I was coming to see you tomorrow," she murmured. "You didn't know that, did you?"

Eric's eyes drank her in. "No, I didn't."

"I was going to say, 'Now look here, enough is enough.'" She turned her head to squint up at him.

Eric bent toward her, trying to block the sun shining into her eyes, blinding her. He wanted her to see him as clearly as he saw her, wanted her to be sure she had no doubts about whom she was talking to. "Enough what?" he prompted huskily.

"Enough of this nonsense," she said sternly. "'It's been two months,' I was going to say. 'Haven't you found out yet that you miss me?'"

"I missed you before you'd even reached the door of my office the day you left," Eric whispered, reaching out to gently trace a finger along the elegant curve of her jaw.

"But?"

He gave a dry laugh. "But at the time, parting company with you seemed like the only thing to do." He paused, leaned down to drop a quick kiss onto the tip of her nose, and added, "Right?"

Isabel's grin was wry. "Right."

"Besides, even if I'd asked you to stay, told you I loved you, you wouldn't have, would you?"

"Probably not." She sighed, caught his finger and brought it to her mouth. She gnawed on its tip, slanting him a sultry look. "And did you?"

Eric felt the sharp little nibbles of her teeth on his finger all the way into his toes, making them curl. "Did I what?" he asked, manfully trying to ignore the sensuous flick of her tongue.

"Love me?"

The words, spoken in low husky tones, sounded more like an invitation than a question to Eric, and they destroyed his beleaguered resolve.

"Like this?" he growled as he tugged his finger out of the way, bent his head and caught Isabel's lips in a searing kiss. He rolled forward and half covered her body with his.

Isabel arched into him, welcoming his mouth, his tongue, his hands on her straining breasts. His touch was like fire, igniting responses she hadn't known she was capable of. It turned her to flame and forever reduced to ashes the walls of mistrust, anger and fear she'd built around her heart and soul.

Just as he was doing to her, she tunneled her hand beneath his soft sweater. Finding there still another cloth barrier, his polo shirt, she tugged impatiently. When it came free, her eager hand slipped into the opening. Palm flat against the smooth heat of his skin, she absorbed and reveled in the feel of him. But when his tongue delved deeply and his leg pressed insistently against the juncture of her thighs, she gasped, and clutched at his back for support in a suddenly helter-skelter world.

Her legs spread in eager response to that pressure, allowing him to settle even more intimately against her. Her blood pooled hotly in the pit of her stomach, and need, elemental and as old as time, exploded. She shuddered, and felt corresponding tremors shake Eric's body before, with a groan, he tore his mouth from hers and rolled away.

She lay panting, bereft because he was gone, yet feeling more alive than she ever had. She rolled her head to the side. Through a curtain of lashes she gazed at the man who had, from their very first meeting, inexorably and—she smiled—often against his better judgement, coaxed her to this end.

The back of his hand shielded his eyes. He was breathing heavily through slightly parted lips. Those lips. Firm, so well-defined. The lower one slightly fuller than the top. Both of them now curving into a smile.

Her gaze flew upward to meet the glowing intensity of his. How they used to unsettle her, those gypsy eyes of his. She'd feel them on her even when her back was turned. They seemed to look not at her, but into her, into her soul, there to discover all her secrets, her fears.

She hadn't liked that. She hadn't wanted him to see through those protective layers in which she'd taken such care to wrap herself. She'd wanted him to believe, as she had needed to believe herself, that she really was as strong and self-reliant as she seemed. Only that way, she'd convinced herself, could she be sure that she'd never again become any man's victim.

It had taken a long time for her to realize that with a man like Eric Schwenker, protection like that wasn't necessary. And it had taken even longer, as well as with a good deal of help from her mother—to get to where she dared risk herself again.

"I didn't think it would be possible for me to ever trust a man again," she said now, rolling onto her side and raising up on one elbow so that she could look Eric full in the face. "It's you who finally taught me, Eric. With your kindness, your unselfish generosity, you taught me that in

ome very important elemental ways all men are not cre-
ited equal."

"They worked both ways, you know," Eric murmured,
'those lessons." He brushed a strand of hair back from
ter face, his eyes roaming her face with hungry intensity.
His hand settled at her nape. "Though I had to travel
halfway around the world to realize what and how much
ou taught me."

"What?" she breathed, turning her face to touch her
lips to the pulse at his wrist. It leapt in response, thrilling
her, and she let her lips linger. Who would have dreamed
she could do that to a man? Isabel marveled. Or that she'd
ever want to? "What did I teach you?"

He laughed, a sound from deep in this throat, sexy.
"You taught me that in some very important ways women
are created equal," he said, borrowing her words but giving them a twist of his own. "Equal to us men, that is."

He sat up in one lithe movement that swept Isabel up so
that she was draped across his legs. "I also learned I quite
like it that way."

"Oh, really?" Isabel wiggled into a more comfortable
position on his lap and leaned back against his chest.
Picking up one of his hands, she casually studied each
neatly trimmed fingernail and drawled, "You mean you're
ready to concede now that we can do more than merely
women's work?"

Eric rolled his yes, groaning. "And here I'd hoped to
squeak past that one without further discussion."

"Uh-uh." She wiggled her bottom as though trying to
get the lumps out of a pillow, movements that caused Eric
most delightful discomfort. "It's a major point in those
terms and conditions I mentioned," she said. "And one we
might as well deal with right here and now."

His breath hotly fanned her cheek as he leaned forward to graze the delicate shell of her ear with his lips. "Personally," he whispered between tender nibbles, "right here and now I'd rather explore the ways in which men and women are *not* created equal."

"Later." She ducked out of the way of his marauding mouth, though she, too, was tempted to toss aside common sense and give in to her clamoring senses. But these man-versus-woman things had been important, no, *fundamental* points of conflict between them; it wouldn't do just to sweep them aside. Or to postpone discussing them when so much—their lives and happiness—were at stake. "Now, behave."

"Yes, ma'am."

Eric withdrew, but his down-to-the-toes sigh left no doubt he didn't do so willingly. The knowledge thrilled Isabel and bolstered her confidence. She loved him all the more, but forced herself to sound merely reasonable.

"Eric, you must understand that I'm neither a cook nor a housekeeper."

Groan. "Believe me, I understand it."

"And that I don't intend to become those things."

"Thank God."

"What I do intend to become is a... What?" She twisted around to gape at him.

He smiled. "I said, Thank God."

"Meaning?"

"Meaning I don't relish ptomaine poisoning. And the prospect of sitting in a living room littered with items of apparel and assorted kitchen utensils doesn't do much for me, either. We'll keep Frau Schultz."

"Well!" He had it all figured out, it seemed. Isabel wasn't sure how she felt about that.

"Unless you object, of course."

"I don't." Effectively disarmed, she grinned up at him. "But thanks for consulting me."

He kissed her ear. "You're welcome."

"Eric, I want to be partners with you," Isabel told him earnestly. "None of this, 'Me, Tarzan, you Jane' stuff, you know? Equality in all things. Full partners." She searched his expression. "Think you can handle that?"

"No problem." Eric didn't flick a lash. "You plan to work then?"

"I plan to paint and, hopefully, sell some of my art. If it's good enough."

"Of course it's good enough," he said flatly. They were silent a moment, their gazes locking, and kindling as their desires kindled, too. They came together for a long passionate kiss.

"What about children?" Eric murmured when at last, reluctantly, they came up for air.

Isabel swallowed. Eric's children... "I'd like very much to have your children," she whispered against his lips.

He kissed her again, but straightened as time-honored values briefly reasserted themselves. "And who'll take care of them?"

At the familiar somewhat chauvinistic demand in his voice, Isabel smiled. She touched a finger to the tip of his nose. "Why, you and I together, of course. When necessary, we'll take turns parenting—it'll depend on our schedules."

Parenting. It was an unfamiliar term and he took a moment to digest it. But then he thought, hey, he'd come this far with Isabel, what was one more new word? Besides, he still had that copy of *Dr. Spock.*...

"And we'll have Eva to help, won't we?" Isabel was saying. "And Delly, of course."

That brought him up short. "Delly?" Surely not even an enlightened man wanted a mother-in-law underfoot all the time.

"If she wants to come live with us, that is. Didn't I tell you? She'd be another of my terms and conditions—unless she plans to marry Marcus."

"I see." Eric paused a beat, wondering how he could persuade Marcus Kramer to propose. "Is this negotiable?"

Isabel frowned, worried. "I was hoping it wouldn't have to be."

"Then it won't be. Come here." He reached for her, clasped her shoulders with glowing eyes. "Listen, for quite some time now I've had my eye on this one particular house on Marine Drive. The moment I first saw it, I knew that when I had a family of my own, that's where I'd want to live with them. Granted, it's old, but it's beautiful!"

He closed his eyes, envisioning the place and trying to put what he saw into words so that Isabel could see it, too.

"It's Tudor, with ivy growing over all sorts of turrets and dormers and such. The grounds are fenced in by a tall cedar hedge, just the thing for children, dogs and privacy."

He paused. "You like dogs?"

Isabel could only silently nod.

"Good." He paused, his expression nostalgic. "I always wanted a dog." His eyes snapped back to hers. "A retriever, that's what we'll get. A golden retriever. They're supposed to be wonderful with kids—"

"Eric."

"—gentle and good-natured—"

"Eric!"

"—easy to train... What?" Aware suddenly that she'd been quietly trying to interrupt, he stopped talking to take note of the misty look in her eyes. "What?" he repeated softly.

Isabel placed her hands along his jaw and pulled his mouth to hers. "I love you, R. E. Schwenker, that's what."

Eric's lids drifted down on a wave of tenderness and love. Just before their lips met, he murmured, "And I love you, *Ms.* Mott."

*   *   *   *   *

Silhouette Romance®

COMING NEXT MONTH

SILHOUETTE®
OFFICIAL SWEEPSTAKES RULES

NO PURCHASE NECESSARY

1. To enter, complete an Official Entry Form or 3" × 5" index card by hand-printing, in plain block letters, your complete name, address, phone number and age, and mailing it to: Silhouette Fashion A Whole New You Sweepstakes, P.O. Box 9056, Buffalo, NY 14269-9056.

   No responsibility is assumed for lost, late or misdirected mail. Entries must be sent separately with first class postage affixed, and be received no later than December 31, 1991 for eligibility.

2. Winners will be selected by D.L. Blair, Inc., an independent judging organization whose decisions are final, in random drawings to be held on January 30, 1992 in Blair, NE at 10:00 a.m. from among all eligible entries received.

3. The prizes to be awarded and their approximate retail values are as follows: Grand Prize — A brand-new Ford Explorer 4×4 plus a trip for two (2) to Hawaii, including round-trip air transportation, six (6) nights hotel accommodation, a $1,400 meal/spending money stipend and $2,000 cash toward a new fashion wardrobe (approximate value: $28,000) or $15,000 cash; two (2) Second Prizes — A trip to Hawaii, including round-trip air transportation, six (6) nights hotel accommodation, a $1,400 meal/spending money stipend and $2,000 cash toward a new fashion wardrobe (approximate value: $11,000) or $5,000 cash; three (3) Third Prizes — $2,000 cash toward a new fashion wardrobe. All prizes are valued in U.S. currency. Travel award air transportation is from the commercial airport nearest winner's home. Travel is subject to space and accommodation availability, and must be completed by June 30, 1993. Sweepstakes offer is open to residents of the U.S. and Canada who are 21 years of age or older as of December 31, 1991, except residents of Puerto Rico, employees and immediate family members of Torstar Corp., its affiliates, subsidiaries, and all agencies, entities and persons connected with the use, marketing, or conduct of this sweepstakes. All federal, state, provincial, municipal and local laws apply. Offer void wherever prohibited by law. Taxes and/or duties, applicable registration and licensing fees, are the sole responsibility of the winners. Any litigation within the province of Quebec respecting the conduct and awarding of a prize may be submitted to the Régie des loteries et courses du Québec. All prizes will be awarded; winners will be notified by mail. No substitution of prizes is permitted.

4. Potential winners must sign and return any required Affidavit of Eligibility/Release of Liability within 30 days of notification. In the event of noncompliance within this time period, the prize may be awarded to an alternate winner. Any prize or prize notification returned as undeliverable may result in the awarding of that prize to an alternate winner. By acceptance of their prize, winners consent to use of their names, photographs or their likenesses for purposes of advertising, trade and promotion on behalf of Torstar Corp. without further compensation. Canadian winners must correctly answer a time-limited arithmetical question in order to be awarded a prize.

5. For a list of winners (available after 3/31/92), send a separate stamped, self-addressed envelope to: Silhouette Fashion A Whole New You Sweepstakes, P.O. Box 4665, Blair, NE 68009.

PREMIUM OFFER TERMS

To receive your gift, complete the Offer Certificate according to directions. Be certain to enclose the required number of "Fashion A Whole New You" proofs of product purchase (which are found on the last page of every specially marked "Fashion A Whole New You" Silhouette or Harlequin romance novel). Requests must be received no later than December 31, 1991. Limit: four (4) gifts per name, family, group, organization or address. Items depicted are for illustrative purposes only and may not be exactly as shown. Please allow 6 to 8 weeks for receipt of order. Offer good while quantities of gifts last. In the event an ordered gift is no longer available, you will receive a free, previously unpublished Silhouette or Harlequin book for every proof of purchase you have submitted with your request, plus a refund of the postage and handling charge you have included. Offer good in the U.S. and Canada only.   SLFW-SWPR

SILHOUETTE® OFFICIAL SWEEPSTAKES ENTRY FORM

4-FWSRS-3

Complete and return this Entry Form immediately – the more entries you submit, the better your chances of winning!

- Entries must be received by **December 31, 1991.**
- A Random draw will take place on **January 30, 1992.**
- No purchase necessary.

Yes, I want to win a FASHION A WHOLE NEW YOU Sensuous and Adventurous prize from Silhouette:

Name _____ Telephone _____ Age _____

Address _____

City _____ State _____ Zip _____

Return Entries to: **Silhouette FASHION A WHOLE NEW YOU,**
                   P.O. Box 9056, Buffalo, NY 14269-9056   © 1991 Harlequin Enterprises Limited

PREMIUM OFFER

To receive your free gift, send us the required number of proofs-of-purchase from any specially marked FASHION A WHOLE NEW YOU Silhouette or Harlequin Book with the Offer Certificate properly completed, plus a check or money order (do not send cash) to cover postage and handling payable to Silhouette FASHION A WHOLE NEW YOU Offer. We will send you the specified gift.

OFFER CERTIFICATE

Item	A. SENSUAL DESIGNER VANITY BOX COLLECTION (set of 4) (Suggested Retail Price $60.00)	B. ADVENTUROUS TRAVEL COSMETIC CASE SET (set of 3) (Suggested Retail Price $25.00)
# of proofs-of-purchase	18	12
Postage and Handling	$3.50	$2.95
Check one	☐	☐

Name _____

Address _____

City _____ State _____ Zip _____

Mail this certificate, designated number of proofs-of-purchase and check or money order for postage and handling to: **Silhouette FASHION NEW YOU Gift Offer, P.O. Box 9057, Buffalo, NY 14269-9057.** Requests must be received by December 31, 1991.

ONE PROOF-OF-PURCHASE

4-FWSRP-3

To collect your fabulous free gift you must include the necessary number of proofs-of-purchase with a properly completed Offer Certificate.

© 1991 Harlequin Enterprises Limited

See previous page for details.